SURVIVING CHRISTMAS

A SWEET ROMANTIC COMEDY NOVELLA

REMI CARRINGTON

Phrey Press

Phrey Press
www.phreypress.com
www.remicarrington.com
First Edition
This is a work of fiction. Names, characters, businesses, places, events, and incidents are either the products of the author's imagination or used in a fictitious manner. Any resemblance to actual persons, living or dead, or actual events is purely coincidental.

ISBN-13: 978-1-947685-93-2

Created with Vellum

CHAPTER 1

SOFIE

I love Christmas, but it takes a whole lot of emotional energy to make it merry. I'm not sure it's supposed to be that way.

Every year, I save up my vacation days so that I can be home from Christmas Eve to News Year's Day so that my little sister gets to enjoy the holiday traditions I grew up with. Decorating the house. Making cookies. Singing carols on Christmas Eve. And this year, I'm reviving a family tradition—making tamales. Hopefully, they're edible.

Bree was only seven when our mom died. Nine years later, and holidays are still hard for Dad. He participates in what we do and is generous with gifts for me and my sister, but he's not festive.

I consider it my job to make sure my family has a merry Christmas.

Squinting, I turn the wipers up another click. This rain is awful. And as cold as it is, I'm worried about ice. That doesn't really happen here, but apparently Mother Nature didn't get the memo.

My phone rings, and I press a button on my steering wheel to answer. "Hey, Bree. I'm only about twenty minutes away. I think. It would be like five minutes if it weren't for this awful weather."

"Dad's pacing. He's worried about you." She closes a door. "Did you get the stuff?"

"Yep. We'll cook the pork roasts overnight tonight. Then make everything tomorrow."

"Awesome. This is a great idea. You have the recipe Mom used?"

"It's in her cookbook. She learned to make them from Dad's mom, who learned to make them from her mom. And so on. I'm excited. Does Dad know?"

"Nope. I didn't tell him. Think he'll be upset?"

I hope not, but it's a risk I'm willing to take. Mom worked so hard learning to make them. I want to carry on the tradition. "No. It will stir up memories, but I think he'll be happy that we're making them."

"Good. I got all the stuff out of the storage room so that we can decorate tonight." She sighs. "Be safe, okay?"

"I will be. The rain is letting up." I decide not to tell her that the rain has been replaced with frozen precipitation. Tiny snowballs splatter on the windshield. It's taking forever to get home, but getting there later is better than not getting there at all.

There's a car just off the road with its lights flashing, and as I pass it, I catch motion and instinctively tap my brakes. That proves to be a mistake.

My car slides sideways. Shoving my brake pedal all the way to the floor does nothing. I'm moving, but thankfully slowly.

My biggest concern is hitting the stopped car. I turn to watch and breathe a sigh of relief when my rear bumper misses the other car. I assume it does because there is no crash or scraping sound.

Then I remember seeing something move and snap my focus to the grass near the road.

That's when I see him. With the soggy ground, the poor guy is struggling to get away from my car, which is still sliding.

I wave my arms. "Hurry! Run!" When it's clear my screaming won't save the man, I close my eyes. I can't watch a man die.

Motion stops, and I throw open my door.

"What happened?" Bree sounds panicked. Probably because I was giving the same energy.

"I hit someone. Don't tell Dad. I need to check on him."

"Take something to protect yourself! Just in case."

"Good thought." I fish in the bags behind my seat, wishing I'd packed a baseball bat for this trip. "He just stood up, so he's not dead. Either that, or I just kicked off a holiday zombie apocalypse."

"Are you seriously joking about Christmas zombies?"

"The guy is headed this way, but he's limping. Oh my, I can't believe this is happening."

"Stay on the phon—"

I end the call because I can't focus with someone talking in my ear.

The man approaches my door, and I grab whatever my fingers are touching. A bag of chile anchos. Some people carry pepper spray. I just carry peppers.

He blinks and crosses his arms. "If you're offering me chiles, no thanks. But I could use some help."

Why doesn't this man have on a coat? It's hovering near freezing.

Since I hit the man with my car, the least I can do is help

him get to a safe place. "Are you okay?" I toss the bag of chiles into the back seat.

Shivering, he nods. He's soaking wet and covered in mud.

"Yeah. I hit a patch of ice, lost control, and hit that." He points to the large rock that's now partially under his car. Or maybe he's pointing at the wheel that's bent at a funny angle.

"You must've been going pretty fast." It sounds more judgmental than I intend.

"The speed limit is sixty-five. I was under that by a bit." He winces as he shifts his weight. "I didn't expect ice."

"Yeah. The weather is getting bad. Don't you have a coat?"

"In my car, but I just stepped out to see the damage, and then you skidded toward me."

"You don't want to get the inside of your coat dirty. I have a blanket." I get out of the car and open the trunk. "My dad is all about safety. And since I drive several hours when I come home to the ranch, he put together a kit. Honestly, I never thought I'd need this blanket." I hand him the thermal blanket, then pocket the can of pepper spray that's in the kit. Maybe the trunk isn't the best place for that.

"Thanks." He wraps the blanket around his shoulders. "And please don't use that pepper spray on me. My day is bad enough already."

"As long as you aren't a serial killer disguised as a big-city guy, I won't need it. Where were you headed?" This road isn't heavily traveled, and it's not the fastest path to anywhere. So I'm curious.

"I promise I'm just a big-city guy." He pulls the blanket around him tighter. "And I didn't have a clear destination in mind. Home, I guess, but getting far away from my family was my primary goal." He scrunches up his nose, then taps his pockets. "My signal is spotty here. If you have one, can you call someone for me?"

He looks sad, and my need to make everyone merry kicks in.

"Listen, tomorrow is Christmas Eve. It's late. And since you don't have anywhere to go, just come with me. My dad's ranch isn't far from here."

He scans the horizon, which is kind of pointless. It's dark, and we're surrounded by lots of nothing. "I guess I don't have much of a choice, do I?"

I motion toward the passenger seat. "I promise you aren't an extra in a horror movie, and I'm not an evil villain." I flash a smile.

He laughs and opens the door. "Is this more like a Hallmark movie where the city guy visits a ranch at Christmas and discovers the spirit of the season?"

"Complete with the tall stoic father who doesn't say much and isn't keen on the idea of his daughters dating."

"Thanks for the warning."

"We aren't dating, so you have nothing to be worried about. But if you are planning to do us harm, go back to walking."

He holds up his hands. "As I said, I'm not a serial killer."

"Zombie?"

His confused look makes me laugh. "What?"

"Never mind. Do you need anything from your car?"

"Yes. My bag. Good thinking." He trudges to his vehicle. "And my keys."

"I'll help."

Together we load his coat, bags, and several small presents into my car.

Once he's buckled into the seat, I whisper a prayer before easing onto the accelerator. Thankfully, my car skidded to a stop on a patch of grass, and I'm getting traction, which is good. Otherwise, I'd have to call my dad for help and tell him I ran off the road. He doesn't need to know that.

I pull back onto the pavement. “Yay! We aren’t stuck. And we should be there in just a few minutes. I’m Sofie De Los Santos. Sofia, but everyone calls me Sofie.”

“Jack Hastings. Nice to meet you, Sofie.” He extends his hand, then pulls it back. “I’m a mess. You don’t want to touch me. And I’ll pay to have your car detailed. I’m sorry for all the mud.”

“Don’t worry about it. Where’s home, Jack?”

“Houston. But my parents rented a house for the holidays. Mom wanted to do something different this year. And I drove out to meet them.”

I stay quiet as he stares out the window.

“But my mom failed to mention that my brother was bringing his girlfriend. My ex.”

“I’m sorry. Hard break-up? Not over her yet?”

“Completely over her. I ended things when I discovered that she was sleeping with my brother.” He rubs his face. “Sorry to dump on you. There’s more to the situation, and I’m just tired of everyone excusing bad behavior with ‘but we’re family’ as if that’s a valid reason for cheating or stealing. So I left. And with the rain, I wound up lost pretty quick.”

“Well, I’m sorry I hit you, but I’m so glad you didn’t end up stranded out there all night.”

He shakes his head. “You didn’t hit me. I slipped, trying to get out of the way.”

“Whew. So you aren’t going to sue me or anything?”

He crinkles his nose and stares at me for a second, like he’s weighing his options, then says, “Considering a beautiful woman rescued me from the side of the road, no. I have no plans to sue. A big thank-you is in order.”

I feel my cheeks heat at the compliment. “Well, you’re welcome to spend Christmas with us. It’s just my dad, sister, and I this year. We can deal with your car tomorrow and have it towed to the ranch or a garage."

"Your family won't mind if you bring home a complete stranger?"

I'm not leaving Jack out here to freeze, but I'm not exactly sure Dad will be happy about my bringing home someone I picked up off the side of the road. "It should be fine."

CHAPTER 2

JACK

S*hould be fine?* I'm about to be stuck on a ranch with a protective dad and his two daughters. I'll be lucky to live through Christmas.

Staring out at the darkness, I try to hide my shivering.

But she turns up the heater and adjusts the vents. "Another mile to the gate. Then you can go inside and take a hot shower."

"I can't wait to see this area when the sun is up."

"It's pretty. But I grew up on the ranch, so I'm a bit partial to it. It's been in the family for generations. The original parcel was deeded to my great-great-great-grandfather, Guadalupe De Los Santos, when Texas was a republic. My grandfather bought adjacent land, and my dad has also. The ranch is much bigger than it was in 1840."

"That's really cool."

"Yeah. My dad loves to tell people about that connection to early Texas. Or at least he used to. He's quieter now. I was on the phone with my sister when I didn't hit you. She's sixteen." She clicks the blinker, then turns and pulls through an ornate gate. "Welcome to the Rocking Double Heart Ranch."

I can't see the detailing in the dark, but the rock walls on each side look old. She drives toward lights in the distance, and after a minute, the outline of a house comes into view.

She taps my arm. "When we get there, just wait in the car a sec, okay?"

"If my staying here is a problem, I can just call an Uber or something."

Her laugh rings out. "Um, you can't get those out here. But if you hate it here, I'll drive you to the nearest town tomorrow."

"Hate it? No. I just don't want to be an imposition."

Her smile becomes visible as we roll to a stop next to a well-lit sprawling ranch house. "You aren't. Not at all. I'll be right back." She jumps out and hurries toward the man standing near the door.

Immediately, he starts striding toward the car. Sofie rushes to keep up with him, talking the whole time. At least I see her lips moving. If the window were down, I'd be cold, but then I'd know if I was about to meet my maker.

When her dad gets to my side of the car, I wave.

He doesn't smile.

I swing open the door and climb out, clenching my jaw as pain radiates through my ankle. I hate having weak ankles. I could look at a hole in the ground and feel a sprain. That's how weak they are.

"Hi. I'm Jack Hastings." I hold out my hand to shake his.

He glances at the mud on my fingers, then clasps my hand. More as a show of force and less as a greeting. "She didn't mention that she was bringing anyone with her."

"Dad, I've been trying to tell you. He was stranded on the side of the road."

"And your daughter was kind enough to rescue me." I shoot her a glance.

He eyes me. "Do you have any weapons?"

This is like when I drove through the border checkpoint into Canada. "With me? No, but I have a pocket knife my granddad gave me when I turned fifteen. It's in my apartment in Houston."

He nods, then furrows his brow as he stares into the back seat. "What's all this?"

Sofie inhales, then pastes on a smile. "Bree and I are going to make tamales."

Her dad doesn't respond. He simply opens her trunk and loads her bags into his arms.

Her shoulders sag.

I step closer. "You okay?"

Her head bobs, and she wipes her eyes as she turns toward the teenager racing toward us. "Bree!"

The sisters hug each other. Their relationship is nothing like the way my brother and I interact. I stopped liking my brother years ago, long before he betrayed me. This level of sibling bonding is foreign to me.

"Bree, this is Jack. He had an unfortunate run in with some ice and a rock." Sofie rubs my shoulder.

Bree smiles. "Sorry about your car, but I'm glad you're here. You can decorate with us. My sister is like the Christmas fairy. Now that she's here, so is Christmas."

I grab my bag. "She sounds pretty awesome, and I'd love to help."

When we get inside, I kick off my dress shoes. They are going to need a whole lot of polish to look presentable again.

"Follow me. I'll show you where to put your stuff." Sofie leads me down a hall, then pushes open a door. "You can stay in my room. This room has a private bath, and there's shampoo and soap in there. It might not be the scents you prefer, but feel free to use whatever you find."

I step into the room after her and drop my bag near the door. "Hey." I'm not even sure what else to say, but it's obvious that the exchange with her dad upset her. "Anything I can do?"

"I'm good. Have you eaten? If you haven't, I can make you something after you shower."

I'm more than surprised by how welcoming she is. "Sounds great. I'll be out in a few."

She smiles at me over her shoulder before tugging the door closed.

I've known her only for a few minutes, and my holiday goals have shifted. My aim now is to make sure that Sofie has a very merry Christmas. But to do that, I'm going to have to find some of that Christmas spirit I joked about. Because an hour ago, I didn't much care about celebrating.

But now her smile depends on it.

After a quick shower, I walk out to the living room, smelling like flowers and wearing clean clothes.

"You're favoring your leg." Bree plugs a strand of lights into the socket and grins when they all light up.

"Twisted an ankle when I went down. But I'll be fine." I pick up a strand of lights. "Are we testing all of them?"

"Yes. We'll deck out this place in twinkle lights. That bin over there is full of garland." She stretches. "And Sofie has some of those ankle wraps. She sprains her ankle all the time. Well, like three times. But to me, that's a lot."

"A sprain?" Sofie walks around the corner wearing leggings and a baggy T-shirt that reads *Mrs. Claus*. "Let me see it."

"I'm sure it'll be fine."

She points at the sofa, and I drop onto the cushion and hold out my foot.

Bree chuckles. "Sofie takes care of everybody."

Sofie tugs off my sock and sighs. "It's swollen."

I inhale as she runs her fingers across my skin.

"I'm sorry. Does that hurt?"

"No. It doesn't. Your cool fingers actually feel pretty good." Discomfort is not the reason for my reaction. I just wasn't expecting her fingers to leave a scorched trail on my skin. But not in a painful way.

Her dad clears his throat. "Get a bandage. And I'll wrap his foot."

My sock is back on my foot in a split second. "No worries. If the swelling doesn't go down, I'll wrap it tomorrow."

"At least ice it for a few minutes." Sofie gazes at me, her brown eyes soft like she really cares.

And I haven't seen that kind of look directed at me in a long time. But when I answer, I avoid looking at her dad. "Sure. I can do that."

A minute later, there is an ice pack on my ankle, and I'm watching Bree and Sofie hang garland over the back door. Christmas music plays over the stereo. And Mr. De Los Santos stares at me from his easy chair.

I'm a little concerned that I won't wake up tomorrow morning. Or that if I do, more than my ankle will be injured.

When the timer goes off, Sofie retrieves the pack and hands me a stretchy bandage. "In case you need it. As a kid, I sprained my ankle all the time. You sure you don't want me to just do it?"

Letting her wrap it means that she'll touch me again. It also means I'm drawing unwanted attention from her dad. My decision is swayed by feelings and not by thinking. "Sure. Go ahead."

She kneels in front of me, shoots a look at her dad, then proceeds to bandage my sore ankle.

Mr. De Los Santos never even blinks.

CHAPTER 3

SOFIE

I'm digging through the fridge, finding food to make for Jack, but I'm fully aware of Dad standing at the counter. "Have you and Bree eaten?"

"We did. I made carne guisada, beans, and rice. There are leftovers. You can feed those to our guest if you want."

"Great idea." I toss the leftovers into pans, then face my dad. "I know it's weird having a stranger here, but I couldn't leave him. It's cold, and who knows when someone else would've driven down that road."

He glances into the living room where Jack is balancing on one leg, holding garland up in a doorway while Bree presses hooks into place. "You like this guy?"

"Dad, I don't know Jack."

His lips twitch into a smile, and I realize that I walked right into that setup. Part of me wants to cry from sheer happiness. Normally, Dad doesn't crack jokes at this time of year. His sense of humor hibernates from Thanksgiving to New Year's.

He rubs my shoulder. "I'm not upset that he's here. And I'm proud of you. For caring about strangers. For making

Christmas special every single year. And for putting up with me. I know I'm not the easiest to be around at this time of year."

I wipe my hands and wrap him in a hug. "I love you, Dad. No matter how grumpy you are."

He holds on a second, then steps away and pulls a plate out of the cabinet and lays flatware next to it. "You really going to make tamales?"

"I'm going to try. I need to get the roasts cooking before I crawl in bed. But I'll decorate for a bit first. I'm not sure if they'll turn out as good as Grandma's or Mom's, but I'll do my best."

"They'll be good." He drops a napkin next to the plate. "This is ready when the food is hot. I'll be in the office. I have some stuff to take care of, and I'll call Chewy about getting Jack's car towed somewhere."

"The wheel is bent. I'm not sure what other damage there is."

"Good to know. I'll make sure he has a flatbed available." Dad walks out of the kitchen, and maybe I'm imagining it, but he isn't trudging.

Maybe this year will be different.

I dish up a plate. "Jack, do you want to eat at the dining table or use a TV tray?"

"I'd like to watch y'all decorate while I eat. It's sort of making it feel like Christmas."

Bree nudges him. "I told you. Sofie is the Christmas Fairy."

I set up a tray in front of the sofa, then run back to grab his plate. "What can I get you to drink?"

He shakes his head. "I'm fine."

Bree laughs. "He looks like a Dr Pepper guy to me."

"Then that's what I'm getting you unless you say otherwise." I give him a quick stare, a chance for him to ask for something different.

"Dr Pepper is fine. As long as it's not an inconvenience." He drops onto the sofa and moves the tray into place. "Thanks."

"It's a bottle of soda, not fresh-squeezed orange juice."

As I walk away, I hear Bree say, "But if you asked for that, she might do it. And I really like fresh-squeezed orange juice."

I laugh, but she's not wrong. I'm a people pleaser to a fault. As I grab the bottle of soda, I poke around the kitchen to see how many oranges we have. Then I decide that going to that trouble will make me look crazy or desperate.

While I'm not currently dating anyone, I have in the past, and at twenty-five, I'm not worried about being an old maid. And if trying to make people happy makes me crazy, I'll wear the badge with honor.

Once Jack has everything he needs, I help Bree with the decorations.

While she unfolds the branches of our pre-lit tree, I plug it in, hoping that the lights still work.

"Yay!" Bree dances a small jig. "We don't have to deal with broken light strands."

"Should we add more lights to it, or is what's on there enough?"

"Those are enough. Let's hang the rest of the lights and garland before doing ornaments." Bree steps back to check for wonky spots on the tree. "Maybe Dad will be done working by then."

"Good idea."

The two of us are singing along to carols as we hang lights and garland. Bree drapes garland over the mantel, and I add lights. Then a colorful ribbon. Later, I'll dig out the stockings and holders.

By the time Jack is nearly done eating, we have most of the living room decorated.

Bree picks up the holiday soap dispenser and matching hand towels. "I'll put these in the guest bathroom."

I drag the ladder to the arch leading from the living room into the kitchen. This is the hardest garland to hang because the ceiling is high and the arch is tall, but it looks lovely with lights twinkling. The hooks are still up from last year, thankfully, so I drape the garland over my shoulders and climb to the top of the ladder. After hooking one end into place, I slide the ladder to the other side and fasten the other end to that hook. Then I move the ladder to the middle for the hardest part.

Standing on the very top of the ladder, right above the sticker that warns against doing that, I lift the middle of the garland and stretch, trying to connect it with the hook.

Usually Dad does this, and he's a lot taller than I am. And I'm not about to let Bree try this stunt even though she's also taller than I am.

The garland catches the hook just as I lose my balance. "Uh-oh" are the only words I get out before I'm falling.

But instead of crashing onto the tile floor, I land in Jack's arms.

I'm not sure how long we stay that way, him standing on his sore ankle, me staring into his green eyes.

Perhaps the shock of the fall and the rush of the rescue is messing with me, but I think Jack is leaning in, closer.

I glance up at the mistletoe hanging from the center of the garland.

Bree clears her throat, and Jack goes pale.

Both Bree and Dad are standing on the other side of the room, and I have no idea how long they've been there. But from the look on Dad's face, long enough.

I tap Jack's T-shirt, then regret touching his chest because my mind is now forming pictures. "Thank you. You saved me a lot of pain."

"If I'd been paying more attention, I wouldn't have let you climb up there." Jack sets me on my feet.

Hands on my hips, I stare up at him. "You wouldn't have *let* me?"

Dad chuckles, which highlights the sharpness of my tone.

Jack steps back and shakes his head. "That really didn't sound right. What I meant was that I would've volunteered to do that."

I hate when people assume I'm incapable because I'm a woman, so I press the subject. "Because you're a guy and I'm not?"

Granted, I've probably been sending the wrong signals by feeding him and wrapping his ankle, but I do those things to help people, not because of my gender.

He shoots a glance at my dad and Bree, then focuses on me again. "No, because I'm tall and you're not."

My dad is full-on laughing now.

Bree claps, like she's trying to break up a cat fight. "Let's get the ornaments out."

Most of my family is tall. Mom was tall. Dad is tall. Bree is tall. I'm not.

Jack bumps my arm. "Forgive me?"

"I'm the one who should apologize. I'm sorry." I hesitate a second before hugging him. "I hope you didn't hurt your ankle even more."

"I'll be fine."

"Y'all start getting stuff out." Dad points toward the kitchen. "And I'll make the Mexican hot chocolate."

"That's our tradition. Do you like Mexican hot chocolate?" I stay next to Jack, waiting for him to take a step.

He smiles down at me. "Never had it, but this seems to be my day to try new things."

"If you're sore, you can lean on me. It might make walking easier."

He drapes an arm around my shoulders. "Doing this, I almost forget I have an ankle at all."

I think he's flirting. At least I hope so, which is nutty because I just met him.

CHAPTER 4

JACK

I slide into bed, exhausted but wired.

While driving, I was an angry mess, but then Sofie skidded into my life. And I'm starting to believe I was actually transported into a Hallmark movie. When Sofie landed in my arms, if her dad and sister hadn't appeared out of nowhere, I would've kissed her.

I don't even know her. Only how she makes me feel.

My phone buzzes, and I dismiss the call from my mother. I purposefully didn't have my phone with me while we were decorating. But I can't ignore my family forever.

Well, I can, but my car is wrecked on the side of the road, and I don't want my parents to find it and call the police. There are eighty-seven missed calls and ten voicemails from my mom, two texts from my brother, and one text from my ex.

Why haven't I blocked her? My ex, not my mom.

I read the texts from my brother.

Will: You made mom cry.

Will: Let the past stay in the past. Forgive and forget. We're brothers.

Lynette: I know it's awkward, but I'm going to be your sister-in-law, so you kinda need to be okay with it.

Mom's voicemails are teary ramblings that express similar sentiments to the texts. I could use her messages as a drinking game and get drunk taking a sip every time she said the words "We're family."

I tap out a text to Mom.

Me: I'm safe. I will not be returning. If you continue harassing me with phone calls and texts, I'll file charges on Lynette for what she stole. Just leave me alone.

I'm sending this text eleven months too late, but better late than never.

Mom: She's almost family. You don't want to do that. She made a mistake. Don't be mad that she's with your brother now. They fell in love.

I don't bother to respond. And I probably won't press charges. I don't want the hassle. But when your girlfriend sneaks your credit card to pay for a getaway so that she can cheat, that's not a mistake. That's a huge flaw in her character.

The biggest surprise was who was on the trip with her. And she swears it was his idea, which wouldn't surprise me.

I can't believe I even let my mom talk me into joining them for Christmas. But trying to be the good son, I agreed even though spending time in the same house with my brother didn't appeal to me at all. But it was clear how little they thought of me when Lynette arrived with Will.

Scrolling through social media, I see so many pictures of happy families being festive. So I add a photo of my own. A picture of my Mexican hot chocolate. And I add the caption *Thanks to a Christmas Fairy, I'm feeling rather merry.*

It's true. And dangling that bit of information will drive my mother crazy. I'm not sad about that.

There is a soft knock at the door, and I make sure my lower half is covered before saying, "Come in."

Sofie peeks her head in the door. "Sorry to bother you, but there are a couple of things I need to grab." Her gaze lands on my bare chest, then snaps to my face.

"No bother." I'd get up instead of lying here like a lump, but I'm only in my boxers, and I'm pretty sure she didn't pop in for a peep show.

She hurries into the bathroom, then walks out with a bottle in her hand. She walks up to the bed and slides open the drawer. There's a collection of paperbacks in the drawer, but she picks up an e-reader. "Sometimes I have trouble sleeping, so I read."

"I really am sorry about the let-you comment. I would never presume to—"

She holds up a hand. "Don't apologize. I can be a bit touchy about that stuff."

"Past boyfriend treat you badly? Or current?" I'm fishing for information, and not in a subtle way.

"No current boyfriend. Past boyfriend and I just didn't mesh. We wanted different things." She shifts, like she's trying to give one foot a break.

I tap the bed. "You can sit for a second if you want."

She perches at the edge. "I won't stay long. You're probably exhausted after what you've dealt with today. But I was going to explain about why I'm touchy."

"Sure."

"As I mentioned, this ranch has been in the family. My dad is the oldest of four brothers, and he's the only one who became a rancher. My parents struggled to have children. I was born just after their tenth wedding anniversary, and nine years later, my sister came along. That's a long way of saying that my dad didn't get any boys. But he taught us lots about ranching and taking care of cattle. I can saddle and ride a horse. But it wasn't uncommon to have some temporary ranch hand make snarky comments about what I couldn't do." She traps her bottom lip between her teeth and smiles. "And I can be a bit hardheaded when told what not to do."

"I never would've guessed."

She nudges my leg, laughing. "Hey."

"I expected to spend Christmas alone somewhere. And I'll leave tomorrow if I'm in the way, but I've really enjoyed this evening. The food was amazing. The hot cocoa, the decorating. I think your sister is right about you being the Christmas Fairy."

"My mom died nine years ago. Two days after Christmas. Car accident. Dad misses her a lot and has a hard time every year. But my sister needs Christmas, so I make sure it's merry here every year."

"You've done an amazing job from what I can tell. And I can't say I've ever seen anyone make tamales. I'm looking forward to that. And I'll help if you'll let me."

"Absolutely. And that reminds me, I need to go put the roasts on to cook so that we can shred them in the morning." She stands. "I didn't mean to unload on you. I don't usually pour out my life story after knowing someone only hours."

I touch her arm. "I enjoy talking to you. Your dad scares me, but a little shaking in my shoes is totally worth it."

She grins. "He can be a bit protective. Plus, I've never brought a guy home before. Not that bringing you home means that I…"

"I get it. You dad is navigating new waters." And so am I. "I'd get out of bed and hug you right now, but with the way I'm currently dressed, if your dad walked in, I wouldn't survive the night."

Her cheeks flush a warm pink. "Good night, Jack."

"Same to you, Sofie." I like the way her name sounds on my lips.

I will enjoy the holiday, but I'm aware that when it's over, Sofie and I will go home to different places. Although, I haven't asked where she drove in from. I'll have to find out tomorrow.

* * *

It's early when I slide out of bed. I lead a scheduled life, and often I wake up a minute or so before my alarm goes off. An early wake-up gives me time to work out and have a solid breakfast before going into the office.

Dressed in sweatpants and a T-shirt, I slip out of the bedroom and nearly crash into Mr. De Los Santos.

Based on the look on his face, he didn't get the memo that Sofie was sleeping in a different room.

"Morning. I, um—Sofie told me to sleep in here. I'm not sure where she is."

He leans around me and glances into the room. "Not sure either. Come to the kitchen. I'll make us coffee. You drink coffee, right?"

"Yes, sir. Every morning."

"Fancy or black?"

This feels like a track question. But I brave an honest answer. "I typically have a latte, but I'll drink it however."

"Good. I'll fire up the espresso maker. I've got a few syrups if you like flavored lattes. Bree and Sofie love that stuff." He switches on the machine and fills the water container. "Are you here just because my daughter is young and beautiful?"

"Mr. De Los Santos—"

"Call me Zeke."

"I'm not sure if I can do that, but I'll try. Anyway, I was going to say that even if it had been you that picked me up, it wouldn't have changed anything. I was stranded on that road. My options were limited. Although, you might have just dropped me near a phone somewhere. And I wouldn't have blamed you."

He chuckles, which makes me think I might have stumbled onto the truth.

"But I'm enjoying myself, and your daughter is beautiful. That might have a smidgeon to do with why I'd like to stay."

"I like your honesty."

"I'm sorry to crash your family Christmas. And if you tell me who to call, I'll get a ride somewhere and be out of your hair." I hold my breath, hoping he doesn't give me a phone number.

He steams milk, making me wait for an answer. So obviously, I stop holding my breath. But my shoulders are tight because while I don't want to be an imposition, I'm not quite ready to walk away from his daughter.

After pouring milk and foam into my mug, he slides it toward me. "You reacted quickly and saved my girl. You can stay."

"I wasn't going to sit there and let her fall."

He nods at my ankle. "How's the swelling?"

"A bit better. I can walk without too much pain."

"Then you can help me make breakfast. Ever juiced oranges before?"

"No." I'm picturing the weird-looking dish my grandma used when she made orange juice.

He lifts a machine out of a lower cabinet. "This makes it easy. All you have to do is peel."

I gather the oranges from the bowl on the counter and set to work peeling. And I try to remember what I said last night when her dad—Zeke—was out of the room because clearly, he doesn't miss anything. He wasn't even there when Bree mentioned fresh-squeezed orange juice. I need to know if any of my words are going to come back and haunt me.

CHAPTER 5

SOFIE

I wake up to the smell of breakfast. Dad always makes a big spread on Christmas Eve morning. Trying to shake the cobwebs, I slip out of bed. I was up way too late and haven't gotten nearly enough sleep. But there is a good reason for that.

Last night when putting out the stocking holders, I realized that Jack will be the only one without a stocking. And that's not right. So I dragged out Mom's stash of fabric and her sewing machine. This stocking won't win me any awards, but it's decent. And very festive.

Hopefully, he likes jingle bells.

If the weather holds, I'll run into town and get a few trinkets to put in it. Because having an empty stocking is worse than no stocking at all.

Still in my fleece jammies, I yank on my boots. Since Dad's cooking, I'll go feed the animals.

I walk into the kitchen and stop when I spot Jack standing at the counter. In front of him is a pitcher of orange juice. "Hi."

He flashes an amused grin. "Morning. I like your boots."

I probably look ridiculous.

Dad sets a platter beside the pitcher. "Go wake up your sister. Everything is ready."

"I was going to feed the animals." I never know what version of Bree I'll be greeted with when waking her. "Why don't I run out and you can—"

Dad shakes his head. "I already took care of the cows and horses. Go wake Bree. Tell her there's fresh-squeezed orange juice. That'll put a smile on her face."

As soon as I'm out of the kitchen, I kick off my boots. Then I knock on Bree's door. "Breakfast is ready."

There's shuffling. Then the door swings open, and Bree pulls me inside. "Did he kiss you last night? When y'all were both in the room? I saw you go in there."

I wag my head. "No!" I don't want Dad and Jack to overhear this conversation, so I drop my voice to a whisper. "We talked. That's it. Jack isn't..."

"Oh but I think he is. And you don't have to whisper. The door is closed." She sits on the edge of her bed. "You have to admit. He's good-looking."

"Very." I nod toward the door. "But he's just here for the holiday. Then he'll go back to his life."

"Whatever." She stands and stretches, then walks to the door. "Sorry we walked in when he was about to kiss you."

I don't get a chance to respond before she's on her way to the kitchen. But if I'm honest, I'm a little sorry too.

When I catch up to her, breakfast is on the table in the dining room, and Jack is setting glasses near each plate. His T-shirt is snug on his shoulders, and I take a second to admire the view. Until Dad bumps my shoulder.

"What?" I turn the roaster to the lowest setting to keep the roasts warm until I'm ready to shred the pork.

Dad is more animated than he's been in a while during this time of year. "When I go back out to the barn, I'll see if

Jack wants to help me. We might need to scrounge him up some boots. Those fancy shoes he was wearing last night won't survive out there."

"Dad, he turned an ankle. Be kind to him."

He grins, then carries his coffee mug toward the table. And I follow.

Jack pulls out my chair as I approach. "Bree said that this is where you normally sit."

"Thanks." I ease into the seat and take a sip of the orange juice. "This is really good. Thank you."

He looks pleased, and that satisfied smile makes my synapses fire in funny ways.

Bree sits across from me in her normal spot, then points to the chair beside me. "You can sit there, Jack."

He drops into his seat, then glances at my dad at the head of the table. "This looks really good, sir. I mean Zeke."

"Glad you could join us." Dad says the blessing, then smiles. "Dig in, everyone."

I'm not sure if having company is what has Dad in a rare mood or if it's that the company is a guy who's roughly my age, single, and handsome. Whatever the reason, I'm happy about it.

* * *

DAD'S LOOKING at his phone as I'm gathering plates from the table.

"Everything okay?" I stop beside his chair. That look on his face signals that everything is not actually okay.

He sets his phone down. "Weather is supposed to get bad. The chance of freezing precipitation starts increasing in about two hours."

"Oh, then I should run. I want to get a few things from

the store." I hesitate before hurrying to my room. "Are you concerned?"

"Propane tank is nearly full, and the generator works, so we'll be fine." Dad steals a side glance at Jack who is loading the dishwasher. "But as far as town, we'll all go. I want to be sure we have enough in the way of groceries. And we'll need more salt so that we don't injure ourselves stepping out onto our porch."

The threat of inclement weather always causes a cautious buzz of excitement. There is a chance we'll only get rain and chilly weather. Or even nothing at all. But after being iced in for over a week a few years back, we don't ignore the warnings because there is a possibility that we won't be able to leave the ranch for several days.

"I'll get dressed." In the kitchen, I set the dishes beside the sink and lean on the counter by Jack. "It looks like the weather is supposed to get bad in a few hours, possibly snow, so we're going to make a quick run into town to stock up on a few things. We'll leave in about fifteen minutes."

Bree squeals. "We're going to have a white Christmas!"

"Sounds good. The store part, I mean. As soon as I finish this, I'll throw on warm clothes." Jack leans closer as he continues to load dishes. "Is there a worry we'll lose power?"

"Dad had a generator put in a while back. And we have plenty of propane to keep the house lit and warm." I bump his shoulder. "I'll finish this so you can change."

"You going to the store in that?" He winks.

His admiring look has my cheeks heating. "No, and I think you'll be cold in that thin T-shirt. Oh! How's your ankle this morning?"

He gives a one-shoulder shrug. "Not horrible." After loading the last few pieces of flatware, he washes his hands. "I'll go add some layers over my T-shirt so I won't be cold."

No more checking out his muscular frame for a while.

Twenty minute later, we're walking toward Dad's truck, and Bree shouts, "Shotgun!"

Some days, I love my sister more than others.

Jack opens the back door and holds out his hand, and I'm instantly glad my gloves are still in my pocket.

His hand is warm, strong. And he's still holding my fingers after I'm seated. He opens his mouth like he's about to say something, then glances at my dad sliding in behind the wheel. Then Jack whispers, "I'll tell you later."

Never before have I been so keen on having the power to fast forward time.

At the end of the driveway, Dad looks both ways, then turns left.

I lean closer to Jack. "To the right, there is a tiny town about ten minutes down the road, but they don't have a lot of options when it comes to shopping. Mainly, a dollar place and a gas station. So we're headed to Stadtburg. It's about a thirty-minute drive, but they have a small mom-and-pop shop where we can get groceries and other fun stuff, and the town has a hardware and feed store. Those two places should suffice for today."

Bree turns around in her seat. "And it has a fabulous donut shop."

"It closes early on Christmas Eve, I think." I search up Sweets on my phone to check the hours. "It does. At noon."

Bree glances at Dad, and he nods. Sweets will be our first stop.

Jack's smile makes it clear that he's picked up on the fact that Dad will do anything for his girls. He was like this before Mom died. And after, it only intensified.

Amazingly, Bree hasn't turned out to be rotten. And I don't think I have either.

CHAPTER 6

JACK

Watching the way Zeke treats his daughters, I'm beginning to question if my parents ever loved me. There is no question about how he feels. And it's not just indulgence. At the donut shop, he asked what I wanted, then ordered. But it was obvious based on Sofie and Bree's expressions that he bought what they like.

It makes me miss what I never had.

He rolls to a stop in front of the mom-and-pop shop, and I reach for the handle.

"Jack, you're coming with me. Sofie and Bree, I'll be back in about twenty minutes or so." Zeke tips his head toward the passenger seat. "But you don't have to ride back there."

After Bree gets out, I take her spot. "We headed to the hardware store?"

"Yep."

We're quiet for a few seconds, but it's the kind of quiet that prickles your skin and makes you shift in your seat. So I say, "Were they able to tow my car? Have you heard anything?"

"Chewy has it at his shop. He said he'd call after Christmas."

"Good. Thanks. I appreciate that you haven't run me off. And this will sound sappy, but it's obvious y'all care about each other, and that's making my holidays brighter." This is probably not the way to impress a man who has ranched all his life, but I can't help myself. I've slipped into a different reality, and I like it.

He parks and stares through the windshield while the engine idles. "I'm sorry you haven't experienced this. My girls are special, and I'd do anything for them. And I don't want to see either of them hurt." His gaze snaps to me. "Don't confuse liking the way a family Christmas feels with liking someone."

"Of course." I nod, then shake my head. "I won't."

That's my warning not to let my feelings steamroll my logic.

"Good. Come on. We need to get you a pair of boots."

When we walk inside, the man at the counter waves. "Zeke, I have the salt you called about. Ready for me to load?"

"Thanks, Sutton. I want to get him some boots. This is Jack, Sofie's friend." Zeke pats my shoulder.

Sutton shakes my hand. "Nice to meet you. Boots are just this way." He leads us down an aisle, then turns around when the bell over the door jingles. "Let me know if you need anything. Today has been busy. Everyone shopping before the storm."

Zeke looks at my tennis shoes, which I'm extra glad I packed. "Eleven?"

"Yes." I scan boxes, looking for my size.

He points at two different boots. "I'd recommend either of these."

I pick up the boot and peek at the price tag on the sole. Affording it isn't a concern, but I'm not in the habit of buying anything without knowing the cost. There is a bench conveniently placed, so I sit and slip off my shoe. Hopefully, my ankle won't be angry about shoe shopping.

This is my first time wearing boots, so Zeke explains what constitutes a good fit. After walking a few paces in each pair, I make a choice.

He checks the time. "Good. Let's go so we can be back at the ranch before the temperatures drop."

At the front counter, I set the box down and pull out my wallet.

Zeke shakes his head. "I'm getting these."

"Thank you. I didn't expect that."

He pays Sutton, then hands me the box. "Want me to drive around back to load the salt?"

"It's on porch on that side of the building. I can..." He surveys the small crowd shopping.

"We've got it. Stay safe."

Sutton smiles. "Thanks."

Zeke pulls up near the porch, and I hop out to help. I'm babying my ankle a little, but I'm not going to let Sofie's dad load this stuff alone. Even though I work out every morning, he's still probably in better shape than I'm in. But I want the man to like me because my feelings for Sofie have less to do with merriness and mistletoe and everything to do with the sparkle in her eyes and the smile on her face.

But I'm still determined to take this slow.

Once we have the five bags loaded, we go back to the other store.

"If you see foods you like, grab it. We're stocking up for a few days." He grabs a handheld basket. "I'll find you and the girls in a bit."

I pick up another basket and walk around the store, trying to figure out what I should contribute. Thankfully, I have gifts. Granted, when I bought the gift cards, I wasn't thinking of them, but I'd rather they have them than my family. Walking aimlessly and not knowing what to get, I think of the fancy boards with all the different foods that my admin, who also happens to be my neighbor, always brings to office parties. So I do what I often do when I need something. I call her.

Hannah picks up after the third ring. "Are you okay?"

"Yes, why?"

"Duh. Because you're with your family, three people who don't seem to care about your feelings." She sighs. "Let me guess. Will is rubbing the affair in your face."

"Did you know he was bringing Lynette to Christmas?"

"No! He didn't!" She sounds genuinely shocked. "You know what, you should just drive back to Houston. My friends and I are going to watch movies and then crash here. Tomorrow, we'll cook and enjoy yummy food. Don't subject yourself to their selfishness. Seriously."

"I only have a minute before I need to ask you something, so I'll give you the condensed version. Main points. I'm not with my family. I left and ended up wrecking my car. But a woman stopped to help, and I'm spending Christmas with her family."

"That's so sweet. It's like the lady who accidentally texted that teenager about Thanksgiving, and then invited him to join them even though it was the wrong number. Do you know that he celebrates Thanksgiving with her family every year now?"

"This is a bit different. The woman is, I'd guess, mid-twenties. Stunning. And her family is her rancher dad and teenaged sister."

"Jack!" Hannah giggles. "You have to text me updates."

"I will. But I need your help. I'm at the store, and I wanted to get the stuff to make one of those fancy boards you make for parties."

"Charcuterie. Great idea!"

We switch to video chat. I put my one working earbud in, and for the next ten minutes she tells me what to get. I'm surprised the store carried big wooden cutting boards, but that's the final piece that'll make this awesome.

"Thanks, Hannah. And you're right." I mumble the last words, more to make her laugh than to prevent her from hearing them.

Her laugh rings out. "Of course I am."

"Merry Christmas."

"You too, and don't forget to update me." Cheers sound in the background, and she adds, "And maybe a picture if you can swing it."

"Creeper." Laughing, I end the call.

Hannah has worked with me since I started my company, and she treats me more like family than my blood relations.

I spot Sofie checking out, so I go through another lane. I don't want her hassling me about paying for these groceries.

Once we're all back at the truck, we load the bags, then climb in. Bree takes shotgun without calling it, and I have no problem with that. But honestly, I feel a bit like a kid since I'm excited about sitting next to a girl.

But I am.

Zeke turns out of the lot but drives in the opposite direction of the ranch. Then in answer to my unasked question, he says, "One more stop. I want to check on Reuben. Hopefully he's closed."

I glance at Sofie for an explanation.

"Reuben is my uncle. He owns the local barbecue place." She shifts her hand on the seat until her fingertips are touching mine. "Really good barbecue."

When we walk in, there are only two customers sitting at one of the long tables.

Zeke steps up to the counter. "Hello, Amanda. I'm surprised y'all are open."

Sofie whispers, "Amanda is my dad's cousin."

Amanda sighs. "Reuben is determined to stay open until we sell out. We had a small rush when we first opened and it looked like we might actually sell out, but now, it's slow. Because people are going home." She rolls her eyes. "But he doesn't listen to me. He's in the back. Want me to get him?"

Zeke shakes his head. "Don't bother him. How much brisket do you have left?"

She looks at what's in the warmer. "Seven pounds, I'd guess."

"I'll take it." He scans the sides. "And some of the ribs."

The cousin sets to work slicing brisket, and after packaging it all up, she adds a large container of green beans and a bag of sliced bread. The total she rattles off sounds much too low for what he's getting and when he lifts his eyebrows, she gives him a different number.

She glances toward the back. "I appreciate this."

Zeke hands one bag to me, then picks up the other. "Get home before the roads get nasty. And tell that brother of mine that he has a thirty-minute drive, and I'll be mad if he injures himself driving in bad weather."

Amanda laughs. "I'll tell him. But he won't listen."

If I had to guess, Zeke is the oldest of the brothers. At least he acts like it. It's also obvious that he takes care of the ones he loves.

The drive home feels very long with the smell of barbecue filling the cab of the truck. Even though I ate a big breakfast, I'm hungry again.

CHAPTER 7

SOFIE

Jack devours barbecue at the end of the counter while I shred pork. The chili pods are boiling, and now that I'm actually starting the tamale-making process, I'm worried about doing everything right. There are so many memories tied up in the process. I'll be lucky to get through today without crying.

Once the roasts are shredded, I pull out a large pot. Working my way down the recipe, I set out ingredients.

Bree taps my shoulder. "Hey. I'm here. Tell me what to do."

"I'll set you to work on the ancho chiles. I've boiled them, so they're soft. But now we make a paste to add to the meat." I show her how to blend them, then strain them so that we end up with a dark red chili paste.

Working together, we add seasonings to the pan. The smell draws Jack and Dad into the kitchen.

"You've started." Dad puts one arm around Bree and the other around me. "This house smells amazing. I'll get the *ojas* soaking." He pulls an old aluminum bowl out of the top of the pantry and lays corn husks in it before adding hot water.

With the meat seasoned, I move on to mixing the masa. Yesterday morning, I watched a lady grind the corn after I ordered.

Bree pokes at the corn masa. "Is this what we put on the husks?"

"We have to mix it first. Grandma did it by hand. But Mom used her stand-up mixer." I spin around, trying to remember where I stored that thing. "It'll be handy to have down if we want to make cookies later."

Jack appears next to me. "How can I help?"

I'm opening cabinets and looking at the pantry shelves. "I can't remember where I put it."

Bree clears her throat. "Um, you mean this?"

The mixer is on the counter, hidden under a quilted cover.

She yanks off the cover. "Dad got it down for me a few weeks ago when I started baking."

I show her the recipe and watch as she blends the masa until it's smooth and just the right color.

Dad has retreated back to his office, and I'm guessing he'll be in and out of the kitchen today. Not because he's busy with work, but because he's missing Mom more than normal.

A hand slides across my back, and I whip my head around to see Jack beside me.

"You made these with your mom every year?"

"I did. Bree helped too."

Bree stops the mixer and lowers the bowl. When she looks my way, tears brim in her eyes. "It looks just like I remember."

I slide my hands down the front of my apron, composing myself. "Now for the fun part. Assembling."

After covering the table with a plastic tablecloth, I set the soaked husks, the masa, and the meat out. Then I set up a TV tray and cookie sheet so that we have a place to put the tamales after folding them.

As I survey the setup to make sure I haven't forgotten anything, Feliz Navidad starts playing over the stereo. Then Dad appears in the doorway. "Let's do this."

Bree wraps her arms around Dad, and he kisses the top of her head.

Without really thinking, I lean against Jack. "Mom always kicked off the making with that song. It put us all in the holiday spirit."

His fingers brush mine. "She'd love that y'all are making them, I think."

I clasp his hand. "She would. And she would've loved having you here for the holiday. She's definitely smiling down on us today."

Jack's smile is tender. "Tell me what to do."

We settle at the table and split into pairs. I show Jack how to find the smooth side of the husk and spread a thin layer of masa. Dad shows Bree how to add meat and fold up the tamale.

Soon, we are working like a well-oiled machine.

When the cookie sheet is full, I carry it to the counter and set out an empty one. "Should I cook these now or wait until tonight?"

Jack doesn't wait for anyone else to answer. "Now."

Bree laughs. "What he said. And how many are we making?"

"This is about five dozen. I'm guessing we'll end up with ten or twelve dozen." I wave Bree over so that she can see how to arrange the pot for cooking.

Dad and Jack keep working on assembly.

"Thanks, Sofie. This has been the best Christmas Eve in a long time, and we are only halfway through the day. But I'm worried Jack might explode from all that he's eating." She giggles and bumps her hip against mine. "It doesn't feel weird having him here."

She's summarized my feelings perfectly.

"You're right." I gaze at Jack, wondering if I'm being played or if there is actually a spark.

I don't know him. He could be a total player, aiming to add me to his list of conquests. But nothing about Jack gives off the impression. The story he told me about his family made me sad. And I don't think he was making it up.

He turns and catches me staring, and then a smile spreads across his face. Every year, I come home with the goal of surviving Christmas and making it merry for Bree and Dad. This year, it doesn't feel like surviving.

Two hours later, there are seven dozen tamales in the fridge, waiting to be cooked, and I'm lifting the lid off the pot of hot tamales.

I put three on a plate and hand it to dad, then give Jack and Bree tamales. Looking at Jack, I say, "Don't forget to take off the husk."

He laughs. "I've had tamales before. Just not homemade." After taking a bite, he slaps the counter. "These are easily the best tamales I've ever tasted. Seriously, Sofie. They're incredible."

Dad's grin says that he agrees. "Just like your mom made them."

Bree nods as she stuffs a second tamale in her mouth.

* * *

I TUG on my boots and follow Dad out the back door. "I guess the ice, snow, whatever isn't coming after all."

"I hope it passes us by." He slides open the barn. "If you'll feed the horses, I'll run some hay out to the cows."

"Sure." I grab the feed bucket.

Dad fires up the tractor, which has a trailer already loaded with hay bales. "I'll meet you back at the house."

Beans, my dad's pinto, pokes his head out of his stall, eager for food.

"Hello, buddy. I'm getting you the good stuff." I rub his nose, then drop in the food.

Years ago the barn was full of horse, but currently, we only have three. So it doesn't take me long to get them fed.

I grab the egg apron off the hook and walk out to the chicken coop. Dad has a tarp draped over it to help keep it warm. And the ladies are huddled inside. I don't expect there to be any eggs because they don't lay much when the days are short and it's this cold.

But there are a few surprises waiting for me. I drop the six eggs into the small pockets of the apron, then close up the coop and drape the tarp back over.

"Hey." Jack, decked out in his new boots, eases up beside me. "I wondered where you disappeared to."

"Just helping Dad with stuff." Facing him, I walk backward toward the barn. "I wanted to take care of it now in case it does actually start raining or sleeting."

He keeps pace with me, matching me step for step. "Are you an open-gifts-on-Christmas-morning person or can you only make it to Christmas Eve?"

My back connects with one of the posts in the barn, and I stop. Jack doesn't until he's an inch away.

"I hear a challenge in the wording of that question. Do you doubt my ability to wait?"

Resting a hand on the post, he leans closer. "It's just a question, Sof. A way to know more about you."

"What do you want to know?" I'm thankful Dad took the tractor because I'll hear his approach long before he pulls into the barn.

"Everything." Jack dips his head and brushes his lips on mine.

I fist his coat, keeping him close, and inch up on my toes. I should not be kissing a man I met yesterday. That's what my brain is screaming. But my heart is yelling at my brain to shut up.

Jack threads his fingers in my hair, knocking loose my beanie, and I snake my arms around his neck and press closer.

That's when I remember the eggs.

I jump back, and alarm registers on Jack's face.

"I'm so sorry, Sofie. The way you responded, I thought—maybe I misread the situation."

While he's frantically apologizing, I'm scanning for a towel. Egg yolks are dripping down the front of his coat.

"You read me right, but I'm sorry for ruining your coat." I run to the cabinet and find a roll of paper towels. "Let me wipe it off."

Thankfully, Jack seems more amused than angry. "I should get this coat either cleaned or hidden before your dad gets back. One look, and he'll figure out what happened."

"Probably, but I'm a grown woman. I can kiss who I want." My focus stays on cleaning, which isn't really working.

He lifts my chin with a finger. "Is that your way of saying you want to kiss me?"

"Yes." I give him a quick peck, fully aware that I might have eggs in the apron that haven't yet cracked. "And later, we can come feed the horses again."

"It's a date. Now turn around so I can get this apron off you. It might be ruining your coat. We don't want to get caught with egg on both of us."

I laugh but stop when the rumble of the tractor approaches. "Inside. Hurry."

Jack runs toward the house, dragging me with him. He's limping more than he was this morning, but we can talk about that later.

Outside my bedroom, he brushes a knuckle on my cheek. "I'm looking forward to feeding the horses."

"Me too." How many times can we sneak out to the barn before Dad and Bree get suspicious?

And why are we sneaking?

CHAPTER 8

JACK

I tap out a text to Hannah, knowing it will send her into a tizzy.

Me: I might be moving.

Hannah: NO. YOU. WON'T! You have not known her long enough to make that decision.

I respond with a laughing emoji. Hannah is the little sister I never had, and teasing her is fun. Then I send another message.

Me: I'm joking. Sort of. I hope your Christmas is as merry as mine.

Hannah: I'm beginning to doubt it. When do I get to meet her? And why haven't you sent a picture?

Me: Time for our tamale dinner. We made them earlier today. Then we're going to make cookies and sing Christmas carols.

Hannah: You did land in a Hallmark movie.

Me: Feels like it. Talk to you later.

Sofie is humming jingle bells as she stirs a pot of something. She's back in her fleece pajamas. The pants are a candy cane print, and the top is bright red. The color looks good on her.

I'm aware that I've stared too long when Zeke clears his throat. He's standing on the other side of the room, staring at me. After a second, his stern expression softens into a smile.

To me, that looks like acceptance. I hope.

"It's ready. Bree already set the table." She flashes a grin at her dad. "Are you going to decorate cookies with us after we eat?"

"Yep."

Sofie ladles beans into a bowl and hands it to her dad. "Take this. I'll have Jack help me with the rice."

He leaves, and we're alone for a second. "How often do horses usually eat?"

"Three to five times a day." Her cheeks flush as she spoons Spanish rice into a serving bowl.

"Definitely five. At least." I take the bowl out of her hands and carry it to the table.

Sofie touches a hand to my back as she follows me to the table.

Now, I have a much better understanding of the magic of Christmas.

* * *

Sofie drags a stool to the island, then nudges me toward it. "Sit. You've been limping. After cookies, you can ice your ankle."

After making cookies, I plan to feed the horses. But I don't argue with her. It is throbbing a bit, but my thoughts are too wrapped up with other things to care.

Bree sets down a tray of plain sugar cookies that are cut into various holiday shapes. "I made these earlier this week so they'd be ready for decorating."

Sofie sets bowls of colored icing around the tray, then puts a paper plate in front of each of us. "Decorate away. The only rule is to have fun."

I choose a tree-shaped cookie because it'll require lots of gooey icing and plenty of sprinkles.

Even her dad is laughing as we make a mess of the counter, getting more icing on ourselves than on the cookies. That's not true for Bree and Sofie, but Zeke and I clearly decorate like toddlers.

When the tray is full of decorated cookies, I spring off the stool. "Let me grab my phone. I want to snap a picture." As I get back to the counter, I swipe at the message notifications from Hannah to get them off the screen. Then I open the camera and snap a few photos.

These pictures are for sure going up on my socials.

Bree runs around the counter, dragging her dad with her. "Let's all take a selfie."

Sofie presses in close and when all our faces are in the frame, I click the button. I will not be posting this photo, but I will send it to Hannah. Later.

Right now, there are hungry horses waiting.

I help clean up the counter, then pull on a sweatshirt and yank on my boots. Okay, so I don't yank. I slide them on gently because my ankle is a wee bit angry.

When I walk through the living room toward the back door, Bree grins. "Have fun. I'll just be here staring at the tree and waiting to open my Christmas Eve present."

I think that was her way of telling me not to take too long, but I can't promise anything. Even if there were presents under that tree for me, I'd still care more about one-on-one time with Sofie.

My heart sinks when I hear whistling. If Sofie's in the barn, she's not alone. Unless she's taught the horses to whistle.

I can only hope.

But no. Zeke is feeding the horses. Literally.

"You can go on inside. This'll just take me a minute." He doesn't even turn around, which is probably good because disappointment is probably plastered on my face. "Oh, and will you send me that picture?"

"Sure thing." I can only hope that the horses will want a midnight snack.

Inside, I march back to my room to peel off the extra layer and take off my boots.

Sofie is leaning over an open dresser drawer in my room. Well, it's her room, but I'm using it.

She spins around and hugs a set of plaid flannel pajamas to her chest. "Hey! Sorry for barging in. I was getting another pair of jammies. My candy cane ones have icing all over them."

I swing the door closed and cross the room as fast as my ankle allows. Our lips meet, and this time there aren't fragile eggs between us to interrupt the moment.

She pulls back far enough to say, "Careful. You'll get icing on you."

"I already have icing on me."

The carols get louder, and Sofie snickers when "All I want for Christmas is you" starts blaring through the house. "I think that's a hint from Bree. We should go out there."

I nod, not sure what to say, or maybe afraid I'll say the wrong thing if I open my mouth. To talk.

Am I being reckless?

Yes.

Am I enjoying the holiday?

Absolutely.

Do I want to keep feeding the horses even when the holiday is over?

I do.

Obviously, not literally.

Hopefully, Sofie feels the same way.

Knowing where she lives would really help with that. Why do I keep forgetting to ask?

Zeke is sitting on the floor in front of the sofa.

Bree is wearing a Santa hat and bouncing on the balls of her feet.

I take a seat on the floor.

"Come on, Sofie. We're waiting."

"Hold your horses. I'll be there in a second."

Now, anytime I hear the word horses, I think about kissing Sofie. It's a weird word association.

She hurries in, wearing the plaid pajamas, and drops down beside me. "Okay."

Bree hands her dad a present and gives Sofie a gift bag. Then Bree sets a small box in front of me. "We each open one gift on Christmas Eve. And that's yours."

"Why? How? I didn't expect any gifts." The unexpected present has me weirdly uncomfortable.

"Unexpected is kind of the point." Bree picks up a very large gift bag, then sits beside her dad. "Jack, you go first."

The tag says it's from all three of them. I pull the ribbon off, then tear the paper away. "AirPods. Wow. I hardly know what to say. Thank you."

Bree grins. "We saw that you were only using one earbud and guessed that maybe the other one was busted or lost."

"Busted. Yeah. Thanks." I need the attention off me, so I ask, "Who's next?"

I know they didn't get these in town today. Neither of the stores we went to carry this kind of electronics. I would've had better luck finding a machete. But these are new, which means someone gave up their gift so that I had something to open. I have a guess as to who that was, and now I want to kiss her even more.

"Sofie. We'll go in order. Sorry, Dad, you're last." Bree shifts to face Sofie.

After moving tissue out of the way, Sofie pulls a leather purse out of the bag. "Dad! This is… amazing. I'd ask how you knew I'd been eyeing it, but I have a guess."

"Beans told me." He winks.

Hopefully Beans can't talk because if he can, I might have to go back to worrying about my survival.

"I love it." Sofie crawls to her dad and gives him a hug. "Thank you."

Once Sofie is next to me again, Bree glances this way. "It's light. Sofie, did you pick it out?"

"I have no idea what's in the bag. Dad picked that one out all by his lonesome." Sofie sits so that her back is against my arm.

Bree yanks the tissue out of the bag, and a squeal drowns out the carols for a second. "Yay! Luke Combs tickets! Thank you! Thank you!" She clutches them to her chest. "Now I want it to be May already."

"I got four because I'd rather you not go alone." Zeke seems pleased with her reaction.

I've heard of people opening one gift on Christmas Eve night, but it's usually matching pajamas. Now I'm curious what Christmas morning will be like.

* * *

I SLIP INTO THE BARN, and Sofie smiles as she gives Beans his late-night snack.

Standing behind her, I wrap my arms around her. "I've loved every minute of today."

Her smile doesn't fade, but she quietly pulls away and gets another scoop of food for the next horse. "It's been a good day."

It's obvious the wheels in her head are spinning, so I ask, "Anything you want to talk about?"

Sofie nibbles her lower lip. "I know that this is nothing—I mean, these are only stolen kisses in the barn, and I don't want you to think I'm excessively clingy or demanding."

I walk toward her, and soon her back is to the post like it was earlier. "For me, these are not *just kisses*. Say what's on your mind."

"Who's Hannah?"

Sofie saw me dismissing messages. I worried that something was really wrong.

Relief escapes as a chuckle. "Hannah is my neighbor and my personal assistant. She was my neighbor first. But more accurately, Hannah is the little sister I never had." I brush my hand against Sofie's fingers, hoping she'll clasp it. "I updated her on my new-and-improved Christmas, and she wants to know when she'll get to meet you. Which brings up a question I've been meaning to ask. You said you spend the holidays here, but where is home?" I cross my fingers that where she lives is within a day's drive of Houston.

Delight brightens her face, and she squeezes my hand. "Houston."

After that answer, we take the next few minutes to celebrate the fact that we live in the same city. We could still live an hour or more apart, but we're both in Houston.

There is nothing Santa could bring me that would make me happier than I am in this moment.

When we go inside, she keeps hold of my hand as we walk down the hall.

She stops at a door just down from mine. "This is where I'm staying. It was Mom's craft room, and nine years later, all her stuff is still in there. It's bit of a jumbled mess right now because I've been wrapping."

"The gift tonight was too much. And I have a guess who

isn't finding AirPods under the tree in the morning. It was really sweet, but I can't take—"

She presses a finger to my lips. "This is the way we do Christmas. And since you're here, you are a part of it. Just enjoy it. Besides, the look on your face when you opened it was worth way more than the cost. But I'm saying more than that." Her lips brush mine. "Merry Christmas."

Before I can pull her closer, she backs away and slips into the room.

CHAPTER 9

SOFIE

As soon as I hear Jack close his door, I slip out of mine and tiptoe to the kitchen. To accomplish my to-do list for tonight, I'll need copious amounts of coffee. I was smart and ground the beans earlier when we were having fun with the cookies, so now I won't wake anyone with the noisy grinder.

Once a pot is brewing, I drag out all the fun stuff I bought to shove into the stockings. I've planned ahead and the goodies are separated into small bags, one for each person.

And I have a bag for myself because the one time I didn't fill my stocking, I could tell Dad felt bad.

But what I can't find are the stockings. They were in the box right in the hall cabinet, but now they aren't there. I walk around the living room, and it takes me way too long to spot them hanging in front of the fireplace.

And they're full. Except Dad's.

By the time I'm done stuffing the extra goodies in, each stocking has stuff poking out of the top. I step back and snap a picture, eager for morning. But first I have to make Jack's other gift.

Years ago, I used to crochet, but I haven't for a while. What better time than the middle of the night than to pick up the hobby again? Mom's craft room is filled with yarn, which is what sparked the idea.

I pour myself a cup of coffee and wander back to my room.

Dad couldn't have gotten all that stuff on our run into town. He didn't have enough time, did he? I tear up at the thought of him picking stuff out for our stockings, excited for Christmas.

When I first arrived, his reaction to the tamales had me concerned. Because I thought he walked away because he wasn't happy about us making them, but now I think he was emotional and didn't want me to see him upset.

Stopping after every twenty stitches for a sip of coffee, I crochet Jack a scarf. It's a vibrant blue that is nearly a perfect match to his eyes.

Hours later, I weave in my loose ends. Then I nestle the scarf into a shirt box and wrap it up. I'm so tired, I don't even care if the seams are straight.

Arms full of gifts, I sneak out to the living room and put them under the tree. Someone has already been out here because there are three new gift bags sitting on the tree skirt.

I notice when new gifts show up under the tree.

But I'm too tired to check the tags right now. I need at least a little bit of sleep.

* * *

Elvis's rendition of "Blue Christmas" yanks me out of a deep sleep. It is turned up to a very high volume. I check the time, then wipe drool off my chin.

Everyone is waiting on me. I was supposed to meet Jack

in the barn more than an hour ago. By now, Dad has probably fed the animals.

My hair goes up into a messy bun, and I yank on fuzzy socks. Breakfast will be late since I overslept.

When I walk into the living room, Jack grins. He's the only one there. "Morning. You look especially beautiful this morning."

"You've been drinking mimosas without me?"

He taps the sofa. "Bree is checking on the breakfast casserole, which looks incredible, by the way. Your dad is in the office. He and I went out and checked on the animals this morning. And there's a stocking for me on the fireplace."

"You like it?" I sit beside him without leaving a polite gap.

He dances his eyebrows. "A lot. It jingles."

"I'm sorry for making y'all wait this morning. I was up all night, and I thought I could sneak a short nap, but it didn't quite work out that way."

He puts an arm around me. "Just for the record, Bree chose the song and the volume. I think it was her way of hinting that we'd have Christmas without you. But between you and me, I don't think she would do that. Because you're the Christmas Fairy." His blue eyes twinkle in that heart-melting way. "So what had you up all night?"

"I can't tell you."

Laughing, he tips his head back. "You're killing me. Let me go find everyone so we can get Christmas underway."

I stop him from pushing off the couch. "Wait a second. I like this. Cuddling where it's warm is like a bonus gift."

He drapes his arm back over my shoulders and snuggles me close. "This is cozier than the barn. But I do like the horses. I've never really been around any before."

"Wait until you meet the cows and chickens."

"Met them this morning."

Dad's office door squeaks, and Jack folds his hands in his

lap. "Want some coffee? I'll make you a cup. Or a flavored latte."

"Gingerbread please." I tap his leg. "Thanks."

After he walks away, I watch the twinkling tree lights, loving how this year has turned out. The couch shifts, and Dad is next to me.

"Hey, sweetheart." He hands me an envelope. "This is for you. Bree will be twenty-five one day, and I'll give her an envelope then, so don't feel like you are getting special treatment." He smiles, but tears brim in his eyes. And he swallows and looks at the tree a few seconds. "I'm sorry for making you carry Christmas the last several years. Way too long. Your mom would be so proud of you. I'm proud of the woman you've become." After wiping his eyes, he flashes a quick smile. "And I planned to say all this long before you knew Jack."

I sniffle, trying to keep it together. I haven't had nearly enough sleep to make it through this without getting emotional. "I love you, Dad. And I'm glad—" Words get stuck in my throat, and I take a deep breath.

"I know. I've missed Christmas. And tamales, which is what I had for an early breakfast. Jack too. And I think it was providential that he showed up this year. Seeing our family through a stranger's eyes makes me appreciate what we have."

I throw my arms around his neck. "Merry Christmas, Dad."

CHAPTER 10

JACK

Bree elbows me in the ribs as we're staring into the living room. "Did you ask Dad if you could marry Sofie?"

"What? No!" I deliver the answer in an emphatic whisper. "I met her the day before yesterday. Why would you think that?"

She gives me a look that only teenagers can perfect. "Gosh. Why would I think that?" Her elbow connects again. "You make her happy, Jack. But, yeah, it's probably smarter to, like, know each other longer before you propose."

I stare, still unclear how we got on the topic of proposing. "Smart, yeah."

The words should slap some sense into me. Am I really going to change my whole life for someone I've known less than three days?

Maybe. I can definitely envision Christmases here at the ranch. That's when I remember Zeke's warning about not confusing the love of what they have for a connection with Sofie.

But if I'd been stranded alone with Sofie, I wouldn't have

been any less captivated. I also wouldn't be sneaking off to the barn to kiss her. Also, being with her while she's around her family allows me to see a side of her I might not have been treated to for a long while if we'd met in Houston.

"Don't worry. I won't tell her you're thinking about it." Bree grins, then rushes into the living room. "Time for gifts!"

Well I wasn't thinking about it until she brought it up, but now that thought is rattling around in my brain.

I carry two mugs of coffee across the room, trying not to slosh it over the sides. But it doesn't help that my heart is thundering in my chest. Bree had me so shocked with her question, I really haven't had time to wonder what Sofie and her dad were talking about. Now I'm curious.

After handing Sofie her cup, I sit on the floor in front of her.

She shifts so that her knee is right behind my head, barely touching it. That tiny contact feels significant, comfortable.

Zeke puts on a Santa hat and distributes the presents under the tree. He hands me two presents, and one of them is large. When he gets to the unlabeled gift bags near the back of the tree, he holds them up. "I'm not sure who these are for."

"The red one is for Bree. The green one is your present, and the silver bag is Sofie's."

All three of them give me a look that's probably similar to my expression from last night.

"Merry Christmas." I'm beginning to understand what Sofie said about the look being worth more than the present.

In an orderly fashion, we take turns opening a gift so that we can all see what everyone else received. I skip the first round because I'm not ready to be the center of attention just yet.

Sofie whispers in my ear. "I'm sorry you only have three gifts."

I lean my head against her knee. "It's two more than I would've had if I'd stayed with my family." Saying those words out loud feels freeing, like I'm finally letting go of the kite string that's been dragging me in directions I never wanted to go. And I was only clutching the string because it never occurred to me that I could let go.

My parents have money. They just don't spend it on me. They have their reasons. I own a company. I make good money. But for me, it's not about the money. I just want to feel like they care, and this holiday has made it clear that they don't.

Getting a nearly identical set of flannel jammies every year has been the norm, and this is so different.

Sofie rests her head on mine. "I'm so glad I *almost* hit you."

Zeke's gaze snaps to us, and it's clear the part about nearly hitting me is news he hasn't heard.

"She didn't. Not even all that close." I don't want him to worry about her driving home. Or anywhere.

Zeke shakes his head. "I don't think I want to know. Open a gift, Jack."

I choose the big gift. Better to get it out of the way. Again, the tag says it's from all three of them.

I do not remove the paper carefully. A few quick tears make the box visible. "A Yeti cooler." I've priced these and never gotten one. "This is amazing."

Sofie rubs my shoulder. "We wanted you to be able to take tamales home."

"Now I love it even more. Thank you."

The rounds continue, skipping me until we each have only one left. And now it's my turn.

This gift is from Sofie. I open it, expecting a festive flannel shirt. They had lots of those in the mom-and-pop shop.

I open the box, and my gaze lands on the handwritten

note that reads *I made this for you.* This scarf is what kept her up all night. I pull it out of the box and wrap it around my neck, fingering the intricate stitches. I'm shocked she managed to make it in one night.

When I look back to tell her thank you, I'm too choked up to speak, so I give a silly little nod and hope she understands.

When she responds with the same silly nod, I know she does. And, dang it, now I'm thinking about what Bree said.

Bree eyes me as she pulls the tissue out of my gift to her.

But before she sees what's in the bag, I say, "I'm sorry it's not more personal, but I'm pretty sure it's something you'll use."

She yanks out the Visa gift card, and her jaw drops. "Two-hundred-and-fifty dollars. This is the perfect present for me. Thank you." She walks on her knees over to me and gives me a hug. "I hope you come to Christmas again next year."

I bought three gifts for my family. Even knowing I'd only get pajamas, I chose gift cards that I knew my family would like. And didn't skimp on the amount. But thankfully, I think the De Los Santos family will like them just as much, and they'll definitely appreciate them more.

My brother would not have hugged me after opening the Visa gift card.

Zeke gets a gift card to a large store that carries everything a sportsman needs. "Thank you. I'll definitely use this."

I'm a bit nervous about Sofie's gift. For my mom, instead of one card, I purchased a smaller card and something else. The-something-else is what has me nervous.

She pulls out the gift card first. "Bloomingdales! I can't wait to go shopping."

When she reaches back into the bag, I touch her hand to stop her from pulling out the small box. "Complete transparency, I bought this stuff long before I wrecked my car. So I apologize that I wasn't thinking of each of you when I made the purchase, but at the time, I didn't know you three amazing people existed in the world. But I decided while we were decorating that first night who should get each gift."

Sofie leans in and kisses me, completely ignoring the fact that her dad is within arm's reach. Then she lifts the small box out of the bag. A gasp escapes when she sees the locket.

I make a point of not looking at Bree. Because I know she's thinking that a gift of any kind of jewelry is one step closer to the specific kind of jewelry she referenced earlier.

When I chose to give Sofie the locket, I wasn't thinking any of that. I only knew that it would make her happy. And that's becoming increasingly important to me.

* * *

SOFIE TUGS me toward the back door. "Dad, I'm going to show Jack around the ranch."

He sets down the dish he's drying. "Take the mule. It's in the garage and has plenty of fuel. And if you're going by Uncle Reuben's, take tamales."

"We'll take some to him tomorrow." She changes direction and pulls me toward the garage. "I have my phone if you need me."

Zeke makes eye contact with me and says, "Be careful."

When we get to the garage, she climbs behind the wheel of a beefed-up golf cart. This thing has off-road tires and a ton of clearance. It also has only one bench seat.

She presses a button the remote that's tucked into the dash, and the garage door raises. "Buckle up."

We cruise along for a few minutes. The air is cold, but the threatened freezing precipitation never came. And now that the sun is shining, it's actually pleasant being outside.

I give up trying to remember the path we're taking after

we pass three trees that look exactly the same. Without Sofie, I'd be hopelessly lost out here.

"Soooo earlier." I'm not even sure what I want to know or what I should say, but something shifted this morning.

"The kiss?" She shoots me a side glance.

"I liked it. And your dad didn't kill me. But I probably won't leave my cup unattended for the rest of my stay." I'm learning how to make her laugh, and this time it works.

"He likes you."

"He said that?" This is stop-the-presses kind of news.

Her head wags back and forth. "No, but I can tell. There was this guy I dated during the summer after my senior year. He came over to the house a few times. My dad never said a word to him. Not one."

"I would've been sweating in my boots. Granted, I didn't have boots when I first met you. But I do now." I grab the frame when the ride gets bumpy.

"Don't trust me?"

"Strangely, I do, and when you meet Hannah, she'll tell you that's unusual for me. I can be a bit wary of people."

"I meant about the driving, but I'm excited to meet her." She rolls to a stop and points at a fence. "If we follow the fence line that direction, we'd end up at my Uncle Reuben's place."

"He doesn't ranch?"

"No, but the land belongs to all four brothers. Only my dad wanted to stay out here and keep the ranch going. Reuben owns the barbecue place. He's the second oldest. And Levi and Noah are twins, but Levi is older by seven minutes."

"And where are they?"

"Uncle Levi lives in California with his wife and two small kids. I met his oldest once. I've never met his wife. He used to be an actor, but he's moved into producing movies. And Uncle Noah lives in Houston. He's an attorney. And married. But as far as I know, he doesn't have any children. We haven't seen him in over a year." She scoots closer to me. "When I was little, I saw them a whole lot more often, but not anymore. I know Dad misses them. Uncle Reuben went through a divorce a few months ago, and he rarely comes over anymore. We're worried about him."

"Sorry to hear that. He sure knows how to smoke a brisket though."

"I've been doing all the talking. It's your turn. What do you do?"

"I own a software company." I wrap an arm around her and hug her close. I can pretend it's because of the cold, but that's not why I do it. "When we're back in Houston, I'll show you where I work. If you want."

"I'd like that." She rests her head on me, still and silent for several seconds. "The gifts you bought. Was the Visa gift card for your dad or brother?"

"My brother. Now that my dad's retired, he likes to go fishing. That's why I got that other card."

She threads her fingers with mine. "Why did you buy your mom a locket?"

"Because it was pretty. And because the little boy inside me hoped that she'd put my picture in it." I am spilling all my guts this Christmas. "But that's silly. It's just a locket. If I'd given it to her, she would've likely put pictures of her poodles in it. Or maybe just my brother."

Sofie is quiet, her thumb sliding back and forth along my finger.

And I'm on a roll, so I continue running my mouth and spilling my guts. "This question is going to make me sound like I'm still in high school, but I want us to be clear and direct with each other."

She tips her head so that she's looking at me. "Okay?"

"I know it's crazy fast and completely illogical, but I want us to date. To be boyfriend and girlfriend or whatever. Am I making sense?"

"Yes."

"Which question was that answering?"

That smile with the warmth of a thousand fireplaces lights up her face. "You only asked one question out loud, but I was answering the one you danced around. Yes, I'll be your girlfriend. It is crazy. But if I didn't say yes, I'd regret not taking this chance."

As I lean in to seal the deal with a kiss, her eyes widen. "Turn around slowly and look behind you. They're curious about what kind of crazy people are sitting out in the cold."

In an exaggeratedly slow move, I shift and come face to face with a large bovine. "Hi, cow."

Others are approaching in a single file line.

"Sometimes Dad uses this when he feeds them, so when they hear it or spot it, they think it's time for food." She touches her lips to mine, then moves back behind the wheel. "I want to show you a couple other places before we go back. And don't be alarmed if they follow us. Because they will."

"Wait. Before we go, can I snap a selfie of the two of us?"

"Sure." She presses her cheek to mine.

I snap a pic, then kiss her cheek, taking another picture as I do.

As I show her how the pictures turned out, a message pops up from my mom.

Mom: Stop with the tantrum and come back. You need to forgive your brother's mistake and be happy for them. If you don't come back, you won't be part of the wedding at all.

I'm embarrassed that Sofie saw the message, and I expect that I'll have to reassure her that I'm not upset about it.

Sofie snickers, then slaps a hand over her mouth and mumbles. "I'm sorry for laughing."

"Please tell me what's funny. I mean, I could use a laugh at the moment."

Sofie shakes her head. "Her text makes me laugh. It also makes me insanely angry, but focusing on the funny part is easier. She threatens you with not being part of the wedding. As if that is even remotely a threat. She might as well have said 'If you don't do that, we'll give you a million dollars.' It's just ridiculous."

My chuckle turns into a full-blown laugh. "You're right. Forgiving and going back are two different things. Forgiving is good for me. Going back is not."

"Well said." She shifts into gear, and away we go, a parade of brown cows following behind.

CHAPTER 11

SOFIE

Snuggled on the couch in front of a crackling fire, I'm enjoying our family Christmas more than I expected I would.

Jack and Bree are at the game table, competing to see who can complete the puzzle first. They are racing to slot pieces into place, and from the sound of it, Jack is winning.

It doesn't surprise me that he owns a software company because he sort of looks the part. In a cute techy sort of way. He just doesn't have the glasses that go with the stereotype.

The owner part is a bit unexpected. But in a happy way.

I'm less nervous about dating a guy with money.

Most of the time, around friends or on dates, I don't let on that Dad has money. It isn't from ranching. That's for sure. The gas and oil wells on the land funded this house and pay the bills. Dad only ranches because he loves it.

But Jack has seen firsthand how generous Dad is.

Caution sets in, and I remind myself that I only know what Jack is saying. I'm trusting that it's all true.

The text from his mother was confirmation of his story. My ears grow hot just thinking about how his family is treating him. To see someone so kindhearted and tender treated that way angers me.

Dad sits down beside me and follows my gaze. "You really just found him on the side of the road?"

"Pretty much." I drop my voice to a whisper. "I read the note in the envelope and saw the check. I really appreciate what you gave me, but it's too much. Dad, I have a really good job. I'm covering my expenses and putting money away."

"I know. Just put it away for a rainy day." He pats my knee. "I'm going to disappear into my office and watch some television or maybe read. And the horses have eaten plenty today."

I bite back a laugh. 'Love you."

He pats Bree's head and nods at Jack before walking out of the room.

And Jack starts puzzling noticeably faster. And three minutes later, he throws his arms into the air. "Finished."

Laughing, Bree gives a fake pout. "You totally ripped that last piece right out of my hand. Rude!" Then she yawns and throws a wink my way. "I'm going to bed."

She'll be up for hours, calling her friends or watching videos. But the made-up excuse to leave me alone with Jack is cute.

Once she's out of the room, he sits beside me. "Hi."

"Competitive, are we?"

He threads his fingers with mine. "I was in a hurry to be done with the puzzle."

"Why is that?"

Mischief twinkles in his eyes. "In case the horses needed to be fed."

"They're good." I rest my head on his shoulder. "Can I ask you something?"

"Anything, Sof. Earlier, I was embarrassed that you saw

that message from my mom. But after thinking about it and hearing your take on how ridiculous it was—which was really helpful to hear that perspective—I realized that was the first bit of outside information that backs up what I've said about myself. So nothing is off-limits. Just ask."

"I have two questions. What was it like when you were younger? Has your family always been so..." Telling a guy his family is dysfunctional feels cruel even if he would likely agree, so I chose a different phrase. "Unappreciative of you."

"Not always, I don't think. At least I didn't notice. It started when..." He puts his arm around me and snuggles me closer. "Will is three years younger. And when I was about eight, give or take, Will ended up in the hospital. Appendicitis, I think. But it burst, and he got really sick. He was in the hospital for a while, and that was when things shifted. I stayed with my grandparents the whole time Will was in the hospital so that my parents could be up there with him. And when he was finally released and we were all home again, mom favored him. As an eight-year-old, I didn't understand why. Now, I can look back and understand that she nearly lost her son and probably dealt with feelings about that. The favoring made his behavior worse, and the difference in treatment became more obvious."

"But you still got them thoughtful gifts."

He shrugs. "If gift cards are thoughtful."

"You wanted to be appreciated." I say it softly, glancing up at him as I do.

"But money can't buy that. And some lessons hurt when you learn them. But like touching a hot stove, once you've learned the lesson, you don't repeat the action." He kisses my temple. "What's your other question?"

"Tell me more about Hannah." Since that seems to be the one person who cares about him, I want to know more about her.

He eyes me a second. "What do you want to know?"

"The regular stuff. What's she like? How long have you known her? Why aren't you dating her?" I grin while saying the last bit.

He kisses my hand. "Okay, so. I need to tell you something, and it will sound like I'm ignoring your questions, but I promise I'm not. Okay?"

"Okay."

"When you nearly hit me, and I walked up to your window, I honestly don't remember what I said. It was probably stupid. But I didn't expect you to be so pretty. Then my middle school brain had to be wrestled out of the way by my adult brain in order to utter sentences that made sense. And I'm telling you so that you know I was instantly attracted to you."

"So if you'd met me at a party or at a bar, you would've asked me out?"

He rubs his chin, which is a bit scratchy since he hasn't shaved in two days. "Honestly. I would've stayed in whatever corner I'd been hiding in and admired from afar. Ever since my break-up, I haven't put myself out there. But because of the way we met, I sort of had to talk to you."

"Serendipity."

"Exactly. But all that to say, I've never felt an attraction to Hannah. You need to know that. But you asked for info. She's five years younger than I am. Never talks about her past or where she grew up. Not even to me. She was my neighbor when I moved to my current complex. Back then, I was getting my business off the ground and eating a ton of ramen and peanut butter sandwiches. And one day, Hannah shows up at my door with an entire tray of homemade lasagna."

"How did she know you weren't eating?"

"You know how grocery bags are a little see-through. Well, she saw me when I came back from the store and was judging my choices. We started talking. I needed help keeping stuff organized with my business. She calls herself my admin, but her title should be office manager. The place wouldn't run without her." He leans in close. "And she flat out told me on the day she first came over that I wasn't her type, but we could be friends. So it's not a situation where one person didn't get the memo. Same page from the very beginning."

"What's her type?" I find Jack adorable, which makes me wonder why she doesn't.

He laughs. "She's close to my height. Couple of inches shorter. Maybe five-ten. And I have never seen her date anyone shorter than six-six and built like a brick wall. I am so not her type. Any other questions?"

"Not right now."

"May I ask you one or two things?"

"Sure." I anticipate that he'll ask about my mom, and I do a quick scan to make sure there are tissues nearby.

"We've spent a whole lot of time talking about me. I want to know about you. You live in Houston. What do you do?"

I hesitate before answering because the answer sometimes scares off prospective dates. "I'm an oil and gas attorney."

"Wow. Impressive. Houston is a good place for that."

"True. Plus, I like it there."

A log in the fireplace snaps, releasing sparks. And we're both quiet as the fire settles back down.

His voice is tender as he says, "I'd love to know more about your mom."

I grab a tissue, and for the next ten minutes, I paint him a picture of the woman he'll never get to meet. "She was amazing. And I miss her every single day."

CHAPTER 12

JACK

Voices in the hall wake me, and I roll out of bed to see what has people up in the middle of the night. I don't want to take the time to put in my contacts, so I grab my glasses and hurry to the door.

When I open it, Sofie is there. "Hey." She hesitates a second, then continues. "I was just coming to talk to you. Dad got a call that some teens were shooting off fireworks and caught some trees on fire on an adjoining ranch. Not far from where we were yesterday. Anyway, the herd has to be moved, so that's why we're up."

I've never been on a horse, but if they need help, I'm willing to try. "Tell me what to do."

She gives me a quick peck. "You'll be safer here. While I change, if you'll listen for the door. Other ranchers have heard, and a few guys are driving over to help. If anyone knocks, let them in."

"Sure thing." I yank on a shirt, feeling rather useless. But then I make a pot of coffee.

The pot hasn't finished brewing when the first helper arrives.

I swing open the front door, and a tall cowboy tips his hat. "Hey, I'm Parker. I came to help Zeke move the herd."

"Come in. My name's Jack." I nod toward the kitchen. "Coffee?"

"Please. I didn't want to wake my wife, so I left without making myself a cup."

I fill a travel mug and hand it over. "It's nice of you to rush over in the middle of the night."

"We help each other out here." He smiles and turns as Sofie enters. "Sofie, I haven't seen you in ages."

Smiling, she gives him a hug, and jealousy has me seeing green. Until now, I felt like I fit right in. But tonight is making it obvious that my life is completely different.

Sofie pulls her hair into a ponytail. Her jeans are fitted. Her boots are well-worn. And she's wearing a hoodie over a flannel shirt. "Oh, sweet. You made coffee."

I scoured the cabinets for travel mugs. And I fill one for her. "Does Bree know about what's going on?"

"Oh yeah. She's getting dressed. Dad doesn't really like it when she helps with the cattle, but tonight is different." It's obvious that the threat has her amped up.

"I wish I could do something." I lean against the counter, wishing I'd traded my glasses for contacts before people started arriving.

Maybe things I'm not saying are written on my face because she grabs my hand and pulls me into the dining room where no one can see or hear us. "If you were nearing the deadline for a release but there was a bug you were trying to fix, you wouldn't expect me, Dad, or Bree to know how to help. Right?"

When she's all logical like that, it's a bit of a turn-on.

"You are correct."

"So don't beat yourself up because you didn't learn to herd cattle when you were growing up in Houston. And I saw that flash of green in your blue eyes when I hugged Parker. We went to school together. He's a friend. Did you ever know anyone who was hung up on one particular girl the whole time they were in high school?"

"Yeah."

"That was Parker. Completely nuts about his sister's friend. And he eventually married her." She cradles one side of my face. "Maybe later, I'll tell you about my type." Then she makes me forget about being jealous. "And I like your glasses."

Sofie knows exactly the right thing to say. Even if she is just trying to be nice. These glasses are as thick as coke bottles. No one likes them.

Two other rugged cowboys show up, then everyone leaves. And I'm alone in the house.

I step out to the back porch and watch as they mount horses, then ride away.

When I'm back inside, I google *stables that offer riding lessons* in the Houston area. I might not mention to Sofie that I'm doing it. But I'm definitely doing it.

After pacing for an hour, my ankle starts to throb, so I sit and worry. I wish I'd given Sofie an Apple AirTag to stick in her pocket. At least then I'd know where they were.

* * *

A WAILING SOUND STARTLES ME, and I bolt upright. Clearly, my worrying didn't prevent me from falling asleep.

Yawning, I stumble toward the door and let in a demanding cat. "Hey, buddy. I haven't seen you this week. Where have you been hiding?"

The unsociable feline dashes past me and disappears down the hall.

"Fine. Don't talk to me." I shoot off a text to Hannah, asking if she's remembered to feed Bandit.

Bandit would survive regardless because he's resourceful. And he earned his name. And every day at feeding time, he stares at the food container on the middle shelf. Politeness is the only reason he hasn't toppled the entire thing to the floor and eaten until he couldn't hold another morsel.

But if food stopped appearing daily, Bandit would stop being polite.

It's been hours since everyone left, but surely, they'll be home soon. And they'll likely be hungry.

I can make myself useful by preparing breakfast. The fridge is loaded with food. And after helping with cleanup and putting away dishes, I know where most things are. So I start chopping and dicing. Then I arrange bacon on a cookie sheet and slide the pan into the oven.

After a while, I have a feast ready.

I'm admiring the array of food when the back door flies open, and Bree shouts, "Grab me some towels from the laundry room. The bleeding is pretty bad."

Panic glues my feet to the floor, but after a millisecond, I run to the washer and find the neatly folded stack of towels on a shelf to the right. Then I race toward the back door, praying that neither Sofie nor Bree is hurt. I don't want anyone to be bleeding, but especially not them.

CHAPTER 13

SOFIE

My heartbeat is thundering in my ears as I run inside. "Jack, I need your help."

Bree looks panicked. "I asked him to grab towels."

Jacks rounds the corner, and when he sees me, his relief is visible. "I got them." He's holding a stack of towels.

"Help me get Colt into the truck. He tore up his leg." I drag him outside, then shout at Bree. "You stay here. Call us if you need anything."

Jack points toward the kitchen. "I made breakfast. You can keep it warm in the oven."

"Amazing. I'm starved. Sofie, I like him." She's trying to be her usual funny self, but as soon as we're gone, she'll be in tears. Not because the night was horrible, but we're exhausted and worried.

I can't stay to comfort her and make things better because I need to get Colt to a doctor.

Colt wipes his bloody palm on his jeans before holding it out to shake Jack's hand. "Hey there. Colton Reed. But everybody calls me Colt."

And Jack, being the adorable man that he is, shakes the

bloody hand. "Jack Hastings. Nice to meet you, Colt. Looks like you need a doctor." He removes my bloodstained hoodie from Colt's leg and presses a clean towel to it. "Hold this here, okay?"

I'm struggling to figure out how we can get Colt from where he is to the truck parked in the driveway. It took three men to get him on the horse. Getting him down was easier. But he can't walk very far.

Jack leans in close and says, "Sofie, hey."

"Sorry. What?"

"Where's the septic tank? I assume you have one."

The man is not making sense. There is a man bleeding on the porch, and Jack is asking about septic tanks. But because I don't have it in me to argue, I point. "Over there."

"Good. Okay. Where are the truck keys?"

"Near the front door. There are hooks on the wall."

He holds my shoulders, looking me in the eye. "Stay here with Colt. I'll be around with the truck in a minute."

I nod, still processing his words as he runs inside.

As promised, a minute or two later, Jack stops the truck right beside the porch. "I don't think I damaged anything." He throws open the back door and tosses a towel on the seat. "Alrighty, Colt. You ready?"

"As ever."

I awkwardly try to hold the towel in place as Colt pushes to his feet with Jack's help. And thanks to that help, Colt makes it to the truck.

Jack grabs the seat belt and stretches it around Colt. "Buckle up for safety."

Colt chuckles, gritting his teeth at the same time. "You're a funny guy."

"We all have our talents." Jack closes the back door and starts toward the passenger side.

"You drive." I dash around and climb in. "Colt, you holding that towel on your leg?"

"I am, but the bleeding isn't horrible. I've seen worse." He tips his head back. "Just wake me when we get there."

"No! Talk to me. I need to know who I should call. Your wife?"

"Don't have one."

"Parents? Girlfriend?"

"Don't you dare call my parents. I'm not dying, but my mom will treat me like I am. Besides, they're in Arizona. And no to the girlfriend."

"Is there anyone we can call?"

"I work for Miss Tandy on her Matchmaker Ranch. Wrangler and handyman extraordinaire."

"I don't know that ranch, but I've heard of Tandy. I'll get word to her."

"Well, it hasn't opened yet. But it's going to be awesome."

The hospital is quiet when we pull up, and they take Colt back right away.

I sink into a chair, cold and concerned.

Jack shrugs off his coat. "Put this on."

I stand and let him help me get it on. "Thanks."

"Any word on the fire?" Jack leads me to a chair wide enough for two, and we sit snuggled together.

"Last I heard it was ninety percent contained. I'd feel better if it rained." She slides her phone out of her pocket. "I'm not sure how to get hold of Colt's employer, Tandy."

"From what I've seen, news around here travels. Someone will tell her." He laces his fingers with mine. "You okay?"

"Sorry to run off and leave you like that. I know it was rude, but—"

"Do not apologize, Sofie. Seriously. I worried for a while; then I napped. It was such an inconvenience." He rolls his eyes. "It's fine."

"They had most of the herd moved when Bree and I rode back with Colt. I expect Dad and the others will be at the house when we return."

Jack pulls a foil pouch out of his coat pocket. "Bree packed up food for you."

I open the foil and find bacon and a pancake. "Oh, gosh. This is amazing. I'm so hungry." In three bites, my bacon pancake taco is devoured.

"There is another pouch in the other pocket. You can have that one, too, because the hospital will feed Colt."

I eat that too, and as I swallow the last bite, an older woman runs through the double doors and straight to the check-in desk.

"I'm looking for Colt Reed." The woman taps the counter, in a nervous way, not like she's trying to annoy anyone.

The clerk smiles. "I'll walk you back there. And I loved your last book, by the way."

The older woman smiles. "You've just made my night. Who brought him in?"

The clerk points at me and Jack.

"Thank you." The woman hurries over to us. "Hi. Thank you for helping Colt. I'm Tandy."

"Sofie De Los Santos. This is my boyfriend, Jack." I cross my arms, still shivering. "And I feel bad because Colt was helping us. It was dark, and he found his way into a barbed-wire fence. But it was the snapped tree branch that did the most damage. Nasty gash."

"Well, thank you for getting him here. I heard about everything going on. Y'all have to be exhausted. Go on home, and I'll keep you posted."

I hate leaving, but there isn't really anything we can do. "Please call if you need anything. We're on the Rocking Double Heart Ranch."

"Oh my word! What a positively wonderful name for a ranch."

"Thank you for rushing over here." Jack extends his hand. "Sofie has had a really long night."

Then with a hand on my back, he leads me out to the truck.

During Christmas, I'm the one taking care of people and making sure everyone is happy.

Not this year.

Everything is different. I still want everyone to be happy, but it's a group effort. And Jack seems extra focused on making me happy.

And I like it.

As he turns out of the lot, he says, "I let your cat in while y'all were out. He was pretty insistent."

I clasp his hand and chuckle. "We don't have a cat. Unless something drastically changed since I was home last."

Jack's eyes widen in a panic. "Crap."

CHAPTER 14

JACK

Crap is probably what we're going to find somewhere in the house when we get back. "I am so sorry. Should we warn Bree?"

Sofie laughs. "Don't worry about it. When we get back, we'll just find the cat and put it in the barn. Poor thing probably couldn't stand the cold. And you'd be shocked at how many people just dump their pets on these country roads out here. It's awful."

"That is awful."

"Do you have any pets, Jack?"

"A cat. Bandit. He's earned that name. I still can't find some of the things he's stolen. All my sweatpants are missing the drawstrings. Granted, I assume Bandit took them. Either that or Hannah is running a really long prank. But that cat tries to steal the laces out of my shoes. I used to use wired earbuds, but those went missing. Once I figure out where he's stashing the stuff, it'll be like Christmas for me."

She's laughing as I turn into the ranch. "Thank you for being so levelheaded. So helpful. And cooking breakfast was the sweetest. Bree sent me pictures of all that you made. And she saved a plate for you because she wasn't sure if you even got a chance to eat."

"I was happy to do it. And I'll make our lunch. While you nap, I'll put together a charcuterie board."

She covers her yawn, but it doesn't hide her exhaustion. "You're amazing."

When we get to the house, the men are just finishing breakfast.

Bree meets us at the door. "How is he?"

"We didn't get to see him after they took him to the back. But then Tandy arrived—that's who he works for—so we came home. She messaged as we pulled into the ranch. He's doing okay. Several stiches and some pain meds. But no permanent damage."

"Oh good."

I nudge Sofie. "Tell her about the cat."

Bree grins. "Sofie! You got a cat?"

"No. Jack has a cat—"

"I am totally going to Houston sometime just so I can meet your cat. I love cats, but Dad is all 'animals belong outside' when I ask."

Sofie isn't trying very hard to hide her laughing. "So I take that to mean you didn't get a cat without mentioning it."

"No, why?" Bree's gaze jumps from me to Jack. "What's going on?"

"While y'all were dealing with the cows and I was here waiting, a cat started yowling at the door like Bandit does when I close the bathroom door. He hates it and cries like I'm torturing him. To each their own, but personally, I prefer to use the bathroom without company."

Bree swings her hand, motioning for me to move the story along.

"I opened the door, and the cat raced past me and down the hall." I peek around the corner and see that Zeke is still at the table. "Maybe we can find it before your dad realizes it is inside."

"Good idea. I haven't closed any doors, so start looking in rooms that are open." Sofie inhales. "Bree, you check the laundry room. Jack, you take your room and the living room. I'll see what other doors are open."

They race away in separate directions, and I'm left to search the living room without being conspicuous. Is that even possible?

Delaying the hard part, I go into the room I've been sleeping in. I look under the bed and other pieces of furniture. I check the closet and bathroom. But there is no sign of the cat here.

I wander into the living room, trying to be quiet. It's connected to the dining room, where the men are talking, but if they don't hear me, maybe they won't see me either.

After scanning under the tree, I peek under the cabinet holding the TV. No cat.

"Jack, hey! I didn't hear you come in." Zeke waves me over. "Where's Sofie?"

"She's here somewhere. Maybe changing." Why did I say that? She said nothing about changing and when she comes out in the same clothes, he'll know I was making stuff up.

As I walk into the dining room, I see Sofie frantically motioning to me. "There she is."

Sofie gives me a look that screams trouble, then walks over. "Hey, Dad. Tandy is up at the hospital with Colt. She said he's doing good."

"Great."

"I'm going to steal Jack for a few minutes." She tugs me out of the dining room, through the kitchen, and into the hall before she speaks again. "I found the cat. Come on."

"Did you put it in the barn?"

She walks into the laundry room, grabs the last towel on

the shelf, some rubber gloves, and a trash bag. "That is going to be a bit of a problem."

Clearly, because opening a door and letting a cat scamper outside doesn't usually require tools. "How big a problem are we talking?"

She drags me down the hall to Zeke's room. "Bree, you be lookout while I show Jack."

Lookout? Yikes. I was getting so comfortable, and Zeke even seems okay with the idea of my dating his daughter, but now I'm back to worrying about surviving the holiday.

Bree is giddy, which is a stark contrast to Sofie's low-key panic.

But when I step into Zeke's closet and see the mama kitty and her kittens on a pair of Zeke's jeans, I understand. "Oh. That kind of a problem. I'm definitely going to have to buy your dad a new pair of jeans."

Bree pokes her head around the corner. "While y'all clean up, I'm going to go convince Dad to let us keep them." She holds up crossed fingers. "Wish me luck."

Sofie shifts the kittens to the clean towel, and the mama kitty follows.

Then I pick up the jeans and drop them in the trash bag. "Laundry room or throwaway?"

"Toss them. He has other jeans." She surveys the carpet. "But amazingly, all the mess was contained."

"I'm so sorry. I had no idea. And I called her buddy, so I very clearly had no idea."

Sofie throws the gloves into the trash bag, then rubs my arm. "It's not a big deal. I'm just afraid these kittens won't handle the cold well. It drops below freezing at night."

"I'll take this bag outside." I skirt through the kitchen but stop when I hear Bree pleading her case.

"Dad, instead of replacing my AirPods that we gave to Jack, can I please just have the kittens? And the mama?"

Hands pressed together, she is working her daddy's-little-girl magic.

I can hear his resolve cracking from here.

"There is space in the laundry room for a litter box, and I'll keep it clean. Kittens are so fun, and the mama cat can catch mice if they come inside."

Zeke rolls his neck from side to side. "Fine, but they can't stay in my closet."

"Thank you, Daddy." She throws her arms around him in her show of victory. Calling him Daddy is like an extra victory lap.

I carry the bag to the back door, and Bree slips out behind me.

"He said yes!"

"I heard. Your pitch was impressive."

Her nose crinkles. "You weren't supposed to hear part of that. But I'd do it again." She dances in a circle. "I have to go tell Sofie, and we have to find a place for them. And names! They need names." She steps toward the door and stops. "And, by the way, I told Dad that a cat slipped in with all the commotion. Which is true. I just failed to mention that you were the one who opened the door."

"Thanks, Bree." I deposit the bag in the bin, then head back inside.

Sofie nestles the towel under the Christmas tree, where the kittens can be seen but their mama feels somewhat hidden by the branches. Smart choice.

And the mama cat curls up with her babies.

"She's Sneakers, but I'm still deciding on names for the babies." Bree stretches out on the sofa and stares at the adorable scene.

Sofie kisses my cheek. "Fire is out. So unless more stupid people shoot off fireworks in places that can catch fire, we're in the clear. I'm going to go sleep."

"You better. I don't want to find you in there crocheting a cat bed when you should be napping." I pull her close and hug her to my chest.

To entertain this type of emotion for someone I've known for only a few days, feels nutty, crazy, illogical, magical, and right.

And when you find a puzzle piece that fits, you don't keep searching for another piece.

I kiss the top of her head. "I'll make food in a couple of hours."

"Perfect."

It does sort of feel that way.

* * *

EARLY IN THE MORNING, I wander out to the kitchen. I figure I'll empty the dishwasher while I sip on coffee. Zeke is probably awake, but I'd be surprised if Sofie was.

Yesterday afternoon, we ate charcuterie, played games, and drove into town for some shopping. Then all four of us watched a Christmas movie. Sofie slept through half of it.

When I see movement outside, I slip on my boots and coat, which no longer has egg on it. Then I wander out to the barn. Coffee can wait a little bit longer. "Morning."

Zeke stops just inside the barn. "Hey, sorry about your car. Did he say when the part would arrive?"

"He's not sure. But if it doesn't arrive before it's time for me to go back to work, I'll just—"

"You can ride to Houston with Sofie."

"If she's okay with that, then yeah. I can help you this morning. Just tell me what to do."

He gives a lopsided grin. "For someone who has been out to feed the horses as many times as you have, I'm surprised you need me to tell you what to do."

"Um." I now regret volunteering.

Chuckling, he shakes his head. "I'm giving you a hard time, Jack. And everyone knows why you come out to the barn. I'm a little surprised Bree hasn't hung up mistletoe in here."

"Okay. Whew. You had me a little nervous there for a second."

He hands me the bucket I've seen Sofie use each time we come out here. "One scoop from there in each of the feed buckets. And I'm not going to give you some speech about how much I trust you and that's why I'm letting you around my daughter. I do like you, but more than that, I trust my daughter. She's smart. And if she wants to feed the horses with you, I don't have a problem with that."

"Thank you, sir."

"But I'd appreciate if you'd keep in mind that even though she is a grown woman, she'll always be my little girl."

I feed each of the horses, then hang the bucket back in its place. "That would be impossible to forget."

Sofie walks in, her hair tied up in a cute messy knot. She's wearing her flannel pajamas, a hoodie, and her boots. "Hey there. What's impossible to forget?"

Her dad answers before I can change the subject. "That you're my little girl."

She grins as he strolls out of the barn. "Told you he likes you. I'm guessing the horses have been fed."

"Yep. Now I need coffee."

Hand in hand, we walk inside.

The towel under the tree was replaced with a fancy kitty bed after a trip to the mom-and-pop shop yesterday. Those tiny kittens have way too many toys. That's probably my fault for buying them.

While I make coffee, Sofie checks on the family pets.

Then she magically appears by my side as I pour steamed milk into her mug. "How's your ankle?"

"Good."

"I was thinking—if you're interested—we could ride horses today. The weather is nice."

"I'd love that. But I might make a complete fool of myself, and I hope you still like me if I do."

She inches up and kisses me. "Probably."

CHAPTER 15

SOFIE

Jack is nervous as we walk into the barn. I squeeze his hand. "You can relax. I promise that you'll do fine."

He flashes a smile, but his shoulders are still tight. "Okay."

I need him to let go of some of the stress. "Dad mentioned that Chewy won't have your car ready when we're supposed to head home. I know that will make life difficult at home, but I can get you to Houston."

"I appreciate that. A lot. I guess there is a silver lining to having my car out of commission. Spending more time with you is worth being without it."

"I like you too." The sparkle is back in his eyes, so I open a stall. "This is NayNay, Bree's horse. If you can't tell from the name, we got this horse when Bree was really young, and Dad let her name him."

"Bree rode this horse when she was little?"

"She did. He's a great horse. Calm."

Jack pats the horse's nose. "Nice to officially meet you. I'm Jack, the one who's been watching her feed you these last few days."

NayNay snorts a greeting, and Jack laughs.

"Okay, I'm sorry you had to watch the kissing." Jack bumps my shoulder. "You didn't tell me the kissing bothered them."

His goofy sense of humor tickles me.

I hand him the reins. "You lead NayNay. I'll grab Beans. We'll go out that side door."

"I can do that." The side of Jack that won the puzzle competition emerges, and he's more determined that nervous.

Once the horses are in the paddock, I have Jack help me groom them. And by the time they're ready to be saddled, he's whispering to NayNay as if they've been friends for ages.

After demonstrating how to put the saddle pad into place, I have Jack put one on NayNay. He's a natural. And after a short while, both horses are ready for a ride.

While I can get on without using a mounting block, I use one so that Jack sees the process. Then I slide off Beans and watch as Jack steps onto the block. He gets one foot positioned and counts off before swinging his leg over.

I hold my breath as he pushes off. But I had no reason to worry because he makes it up on the first try.

"I'm impressed, Jack." I hand him the reins.

He winks. "That's my aim. Always."

"I'll have you walk around the paddock for a bit to get a feel for riding. Then we'll go on a short trail ride. Sound okay?"

"I'm game."

I explain how to get the horse moving and how to change directions. He walks the horse all the way around, then turns NayNay around and makes another loop in the opposite direction.

"This is fun. I mean, I won't be chasing steers and

wrestling them to the ground anytime soon." He pats his horse. "Mostly NayNay is making me look good, I think."

I swing up onto my horse, and we ride out of the paddock and onto the trail. The sun is bright which cuts the chill of the air. NayNay follows Beans. And I explain to Jack how to shift in the saddle when going uphill or downhill.

While the ranch is a bit hilly in places, there is nothing very steep, which makes trail riding easy for beginners.

Conversation flows as we ride, and time blows by.

By the time we get back to the barn, it's well past lunch.

He watches me dismount, then does the same. And in a second, he's in front of me. "Thank you. For teaching me. And for sharing this part of your life with me."

His look warms me from the inside out.

"You did great." I inch up on my toes. "And, for the record, I've never taken a date horseback riding before."

He slides his arms around me. "Is that so?"

"I never told you my type, did I?"

Dotting kisses on my face, he whispers, "You have not."

"Smart, good-looking. An all-around city guy." My list is interrupted by a kiss. "And tall is a bonus."

"So that I have a better view of you hanging the garland on your own?"

"Exactly." I'm normally cautious and skeptical when it comes to dating. But this man swooped in like the word walls never existed.

It's like Santa plopped him on the side of the road for me to find.

* * *

WE'RE ALL a little on edge as the New Year approaches. Of course we're excited, but the threat of fire has us nervous. I know I'll feel better when the fireworks stop.

I fill four flutes with sparkling cider and pass them around. Loud pops echo outside even though my phone indicates we have another three minutes until midnight. "Some people have trouble reading their digital clocks."

Bree snickers. "That's funny."

The pops become more frequent.

We all stare at the clock, which probably makes time move more slowly. Then we count down the last ten seconds.

"Happy New Year!" Bree holds up her glass.

Dad raises his. "To a great year."

Jack and I join in on the toast. And we all take a sip.

Then Jack tugs me into the corner of the dining room. "This has been hands-down the most amazing week of my life. And it probably sounds corny, but I hope that next year, I'm toasting in the new year with you. Again."

Our lips meet, and the world outside explodes with fireworks.

Or maybe they're all in my head.

* * *

Usually at the end of the holiday week, I'm eager to go back to my normal life. I love spending time out here, but my life is in Houston. This time, everything feels different.

I'm a little afraid that leaving will pop this magical bubble, and I'll never get this feeling back.

While I say goodbye to the kitties, Jack loads our stuff. He also cleaned up the inside of my car this morning, which I know impressed my dad.

We're off to a later start than I was hoping. And it's mostly my fault. We spent the morning playing board games. Dad included. And I was not going to cut that short. Then we had lunch and talked.

Now, I'm hoping we'll be home before midnight. I'm happy Jack will be with me. I don't like being on that highway alone at night. There are stretches in the middle of nowhere, and getting stranded out there would be a nightmare.

Once we're all outside, I brace myself for goodbyes. This is my least favorite part of visiting.

Bree hugs me and whispers, "You better keep me posted."

Knowing full-well what she means, I ask, "On what?"

For that, I get a poke in the ribs.

She walks over and hugs Jack. "You're the second-best surprise this Christmas."

"Second? What beat me out?" Jack feigns having his feelings hurt.

Bree grins and glances at Dad. "Cats." She winks, making sure he knows she appreciates the hand he had in that.

Dad gives me a bear hug. "Call me when you get home. I'm glad Jack is traveling with you. And please be careful on the road." He glances up at the sky. Looks like we might finally get the rain we needed the other night."

"We'll be careful." I hold him tight. "Love you, Dad. It's been a good Christmas."

Nodding, he steps back. "The best in a long time."

Jack opens the driver's door for me, but instead of sliding in, I hand him the keys. "Would you mind taking the first shift?"

"Not a bit." Then he runs around and opens the other door.

He might only be doing it to impress Dad, but it's working on me. And Bree.

She sighs. "Chivalry isn't dead."

And then we're off.

Jack looks at me when he gets to the gate. "Which way?"

I give him directions to the highway. And once we're there, I ask, "Tell me about your company. What is the software used for?"

The lights on the dash make his smile visible, and for the next hour, he talks about his business. I understand approximately twenty percent of the words he's using, but his passion about the topic is mesmerizing.

As we approach the Luling exit, he turns on his blinker. "It's mandatory to stop at Buc-ee's."

"Good because I could use a stop. And I can drive after that."

"Whatever makes you happy." He pulls up by the gas pumps. "I'll fill this and meet you inside."

I hold out my credit card. "Thanks for pumping gas."

He shakes his head. "You are not paying. Not after everything y'all did for me this week. I'll get it."

"Thanks, Jack."

We pull out of the lot forty-five minutes later with way too much jerky and a bag of warm candied cashews.

But five minutes later, I stop snacking because rain is coming down in sheets, and seeing the lines takes focus. Conversation has stopped, and the radio is on low volume.

I can't see where I'm going with loud music blaring.

A semi blows past us, spraying water on the windshield. I click to make the wipers work faster, but they are useless against the torrential rain.

A bump indicates that I ran over something, but it didn't feel very big. I glance in the rearview mirror, praying there isn't a body in the road behind me. "Not sure what I hit."

"Looked like a board."

"I hope it didn't have any nails in it." That's when my warning light comes on that my tire is low. The car starts pulling to the right, and I decide to stop on the shoulder. As I leave the lane, I hit something. Something not small.

Jack blows out a breath. "That didn't sound good." He looks at his phone. "But the good news is, there's a phone signal."

CHAPTER 16

JACK

What are the odds that Sofie and I would both bend wheels on the same trip? Not good. But she did.

The tow truck driver turns into the garage parking lot. "Lou will call you in the morning."

"Thanks. After you get the car unloaded, could you possibly drop us at a hotel?" I'm not sure Uber is a thing out here.

He points across the street. "Only hotel in town is right there."

I glance at Sofie. "Thanks. We'll just walk over then."

He called it a hotel, but it's not. This place looks like it's been ripped from the 1960s and dropped here in the middle of nowhere.

But it has to be better than sleeping in her car. I hope.

"No sense in the little lady getting wetter. Just hang tight. I'll drop you there when I'm done." He flashes Sofie a smile, then slides out.

And now I'm really glad I sat in the middle.

She takes my hand. "I'll wait until we get rooms before calling Dad. But he'll be less worried since you're with me."

"I feel like I should apologize. Like I'm bad luck or something."

"That doesn't make any sense. I'm the one who was driving." She rests her head on my shoulder. "And thanks for sitting in the middle."

"Not a problem, little lady." I wink and squeeze her hand. "The rain is letting up. Need anything out of the trunk?"

"My bag. And then we'll just cross the street. He doesn't need to drive us." She turns and looks out the rear window. "Looks like he's almost done. Hopefully that motel has rooms available. There are lots of trucks in that lot."

"Yeah." I hold up crossed fingers. "But we'll figure something out."

The rain stops completely, and we climb out. I get our bags, and after saying goodbye to the wrecker driver, we dash across the street.

There is no one at the desk in the lobby, so I tap the little bell on the counter.

The other lodgers might be perfectly respectable, but I have no way of knowing that. And if they don't have rooms next to each other, I'm going to worry all night long. But asking Sofie to share a room seems assuming. Even if my reasons are honorable.

An old woman, like old enough to be Zeke's grandma, walks out from the back room. That's a stretch, but there's a possibility she went to school with Abe Lincoln. She's old. And slow, which I suppose is understandable.

When she gets to the counter, she opens a logbook. "I have one room left. It'll be Seventy-five dollars."

Maybe she saw us cross the road and knows we have no other option.

But I sort of want to hug her because she eased my worry

about Sofie. Now I have a different kind of worry, but Sofie and I can talk about that in the room.

I slide my credit card out of my phone case and hand it over. "Looks like we showed up at the right time."

She nods and turns the logbook around. "Put your names here."

Sofie writes our names in the book, and I don't question why she leaves off her last name. We'll let this lady assume what she wants.

Small towns can be weird, and I don't want to find out the hard way if this one is odd like that.

The old woman lays my card on a metal contraption, then lays a carbon copy receipt on top of it. After sliding the thingamajig over the top, she hands me my card and the receipt. "Sign here."

I sign.

She rips one page out of the receipt and gives it to me. "Let me get the key."

Sofie bites back a smile as the lady shuffles toward the wall of hooks and takes down the last key.

"Room twelve. Right next door." She turns toward the back, then stops. "The diner next door is open until midnight."

"Thanks." I hand Sofie the key and grab our bags. "Have a great evening."

"You, too, hun." She shuffles into the back room.

Room twelve is small and has one double bed. Before crashing on the floor, I need food. "Hungry?"

"As a horse." She grins. "Let's go before it decides to start raining again."

Hand in hand, we cross the parking lot to the diner.

A waitress waves as we enter. "Sit anywhere. I'll be with you in a minute."

Sofie slides into a booth, and I sit next to her on the red

vinyl bench.

"Since we don't know anything about this place, I was a little worried about you being by yourself, so I can't say I was too disappointed about the one room. I just expected it to have two beds."

She taps out a text to her dad, updating him. "I'm fine with the way it worked out." After hitting send, she sets her phone down. "And please don't say that you'll sleep on the floor. Did you see it? Nasty. We'll share the bed."

"Are you sure? The last thing I want is for you to be the slightest bit uncomfortable."

She bites her lip as the waitress walks up.

"Sorry about the wait." After handing us menus, she pulls out an ordering pad. "What can I get y'all to drink?"

We order drinks, and she hurries away, leaving us to study the menu.

"Was there something you were going to say?" I nudge her.

"I'm weirdly comfortable around you, Jack." She opens her menu. "Normally, when I meet someone, I don't share my life story until after the fifth or sixth date. And I've dated maybe two guys that long. One of those was in high school."

"Is that your way of telling me I'm weird and different?"

"You're my kind of different. Now I need to see what I want, so stop distracting me."

"Note to self. Be nice to Sofie when she's hungry." I scan the menu, waiting for her retort.

She's quiet half a second, then says, "Note to Jack. Be nice to me *all the time*."

"Yes, ma'am."

* * *

You only realize how small a double bed is when you have to share it with someone. And more specifically someone who has a dad like hers. Not that I would treat Sofie any differently if her dad were anyone else or not in the picture.

I take off my glasses and lie on my back with my hands by my sides, trying to take up as little space as possible. "Have enough room?"

"Yep." She snuggles close and rests her head on my shoulder. "This okay?"

Sleeping this close is the only way we'll avoiding having one of us fall out of bed.

"Totally." I shift my arm so she can cuddle even closer. Then I nestle my face against her hair, loving the scent of her shampoo. I'll miss snuggling with her on the couch every evening. "This is another silver lining."

"You are all about finding the bright side of things. And I like that. A lot."

I stay quiet so that she can fall asleep. What I don't say is that she's the bright side. She's like sunshine in a pair of boots. Or flats. Or whatever footwear she chooses that day.

Something about this woman bring out my optimistic side.

It'll be hours before I drift off because I am soaking this up. It is way too soon to feel this way for Sofie. And I need to be home and in my regular routine to confirm it's not an overload of tamales, barbecue, and cookies that are firing up my emotions. But if every night for the rest of my life ended like this, I'd be a happy man.

* * *

By noon, Lou has Sofie's car in working order, and Sofie hands me the keys. "You drive since you know where you live."

"Makes sense." I tap out a text to Hannah, letting her know what happened, then shove my phone in the outside pocket of my bag. "And away we go."

An hour evaporates as we talk. And I'm a little sad when I park in front of my apartment building.

This is the part I'm dreading. When I get out of this car, everything changes. I leave the happy little snow globe behind. So before getting out, I lean over and kiss her. "I'll call you."

"I'm counting on that." She cradles one side of my face. "Jack Hastings, finder of bright sides."

"I was worried about surviving Christmas, but I couldn't have dreamed up such an amazing week." I kiss her again before opening the door.

After grabbing my bag and the cooler, I stand on the sidewalk and watch as she pulls away.

Then I trudge up the stairs to my apartment.

Hannah is waiting outside my door. "Spill it, buddy. You didn't send nearly enough updates. I'm dying for info."

"Come on in. I'll tell you about my week."

CHAPTER 17

SOFIE

After turning out of the lot, I drive two blocks, then turn into my neighborhood. I didn't mention to Jack that his apartment is walking distance from my house because I want to surprise him.

The hard part now is waiting until he calls me. I'll give him a day before I call him first.

Bree calls as I'm unlocking the front door. "You home? Please say yes so that Dad will stop pacing."

"Just walked in and locked my front door."

She hollers, sharing that info with Dad. "Good. Now tell me about Jack. Has he called you? When are you going on a date?"

My sister is not helping my impatience.

"I dropped him off five minutes ago. Less than that even. He probably won't call until tomorrow. We've been connected at the hip. He probably needs space."

"Nope. He'll call you soon. I know it. And when he does, text me."

"I will." I drop my bag in my room, then kick off my shoes. "But don't expect a text before tomorrow."

"You're wrong. But we'll see. Love you. Bye." Bree hangs up, and I set my phone aside.

If he waits until tomorrow to call, I'll be a tad disappointed. But he has a life and a company to run.

I change clothes and call the law office, letting them know I'm on my way in for the rest of the afternoon. I didn't mention to Jack that I was going into the office, so hopefully he doesn't want to grab dinner tonight because I'll be working until late in the night to finish up today's to-do list.

As I walk to my car, I look at the phone more than once. Checking every fifteen seconds is too often. But I'm eager to hear from him.

All the doubts I didn't have when I was with Jack are pounding in my head now.

Maybe it's just my lawyer brain kicking in.

Hopefully, working drowns out the doubts.

At the office, I close my office door so that people won't bother me unless it's important. Typically people chat about the holidays, but I'm afraid to gush about Jack until I hear from him.

What if all of it was a lie and the text from his mom was just his friend helping him pull off a farce.

By midnight, I've blown through more than today's to-do list.

Frustration apparently makes me productive.

Bree has texted three times, asking if Jack has called. And every time I reply in the negative, I question my choices a bit more.

For a man who had an amazing week and wanted to ring in the next new year with me, he sure is waiting a long time to call.

* * *

When I wake up, I stare at the ceiling, convincing myself to look at my phone. Jack has not texted or called.

But this is crazy. We spent a week together and really clicked. I'll simply call him.

It rings and rings, and I envision him standing near his phone, grimacing and trying to decide if he should answer. Maybe I'm wrong, but whatever the reason, he doesn't answer.

Blowing out a breath, I throw back the covers and head for the shower. Sobbing there doesn't really count as crying because the water makes the tears unnoticeable. But the shower doesn't do anything for red puffy eyes.

As I finish brushing my teeth, Bree calls. I haven't responded to s a single text from her since last night, but I can't keep ignoring her.

Doing to her what Jack is doing to me is completely unfair.

"Hey. He hasn't called." I try to keep my voice neutral.

Bree's reaction is anything but. "What?! Oh my gosh. I hope he's not dead."

"Really, Bree? That's a stretch. He just…" I can't finish the sentence. "Listen, I can't talk about this right now. I need to go to work."

"Let me get Dad. We'll drive to Houston and find him. Something's wrong, Bree. He's not ignoring you."

"Don't come to Houston. And tell Dad if you want. He doesn't know where Jack lives, so it's probably safe to tell him that Jack ghosted me."

"Stop it. He didn't ghost you."

"The simplest explanation is usually the answer. But you need to get to school, and I need to go earn my paycheck. I'll talk to you tonight."

"Go to his apartment."

"You want me to knock on every door in the complex

until I find him?" I slip on my red pumps, hoping they make me feel more confident today.

"Yes. He would. For all you know, he's in a hospital bed, trying to get a nurse to call you."

"I'm hanging up now." I end the call and walk to my car.

It'll take me a few days until I don't think about Jack every other second, but slowly that will change. The saddest part of all this is, now I'll have a new reason to survive Christmas. He's ruined all my favorite things.

That night, I text Bree instead of answering the phone.

Me: He hasn't called.

Bree: Answer your phone.

Me: No.

Bree: Fine. But one day I won't answer your call and you won't like it.

Me: We'll talk tomorrow. I just can't right now. Please understand.

I feel guilty not talking to my sister, but hopefully she'll forgive me my pity party. After maintaining a professional smile all day on the job, I'm too drained to think positive thoughts.

Tomorrow, I'll call her. Tonight, I'll contemplate calling hospitals and checking to see if they have a Jack Hastings as a patient. My heart wants Bree to be right, but she's not.

Jack isn't in a hospital somewhere.

* * *

I GET UP EXTRA EARLY and run to the coffee shop. The exercise is good for me, and the walk back will help clear my head. Hopefully, I don't run into a particular software engineer who lives near here.

It's a chilly morning, and I pull up the hood on my sweatshirt. That will keep me warm and make me harder to spot.

Although, if he were looking for me, I wouldn't be jogging to get coffee. I'd drive like a normal person.

I make it half a block before changing my mind. Driving will be warmer.

And faster.

After ordering, I wait near the wall. My phone lights up with a call from Bree, and I swipe to answer. "Morning."

"Hi. Dad wants to talk to you." Bree does not sound chipper.

"Wait, Bree. What did you tell him? Is he mad? Why does he walk to talk?"

Dad asks, "I need a reason to talk to my daughter?"

"Hi, Dad."

He inhales, then blows out a breath. Whenever he's about to give a mini lecture, he does this, so I prepare for whatever wisdom he feels the need to impart.

"I know you are questioning your judgment, feeling guilty because you fell hard and fast."

Fighting tears—because crying in a coffee shop is embarrassing—I nod even though Dad can't see me. "Yeah." I choke out the single word.

"You were at school the day your mom had that wreck."

The barista calls my name, and I snatch the cup off the counter and rush toward the door. On the way out, I grab a handful of napkins.

I have a feeling that I'll need them after hearing Dad's story.

"I remember."

"She and I were supposed to have lunch that day. I waited, surprised she didn't let me know she was running late. After an hour, I was concerned, and hours later, that turned into full-blown worry. Panic even."

I'm sobbing, so I don't respond.

"You know what never crossed my mind?"

"What?"

"That she'd left me."

I drop into the cold chair on the patio. Thanks to the winter chill, I'm alone out here. "But, Dad, that was different. Y'all loved each other. Of course she wouldn't leave you."

"It's the same, sweetheart. If Jack hasn't called you, there is a reason, and it's not because he's ghosting you. There is a voice in your heart that agrees with me, trust it. Not the doubts in your head. And don't tell me you don't know Jack because you do."

I need to spend some alone time with the voice in my head. "How can you sound so sure? I want to believe he wasn't lying to us all week."

"Because his car is ready, and Chewy's calls all go straight to voicemail."

Maybe after this talk, I won't struggle through my workday. "Thanks, Dad."

"Bree wants to talk to you."

I hear a shuffle, then say, "Hey."

"What gives? Dad tells you the same thing I've been saying for two days, and suddenly you're convinced?"

"Sorry." And I don't tell her that I'm not completely convinced. I'm just willing to admit I might be wrong.

Motion near the corner catches my attention, and I spot someone pulling out of view when I glance that way.

"You need to find him."

I keep the phone to my ear as I walk to my car. I don't want to tip off the creeper and let them know they've been spotted. "I'm not sure how to do that. I could go to the spot where I dropped him off and shout his name at the top of my lungs."

"Sounds reasonable to me." She laughs. "I'm joking, but seriously, think. Where does he work? You could go there."

"I can tell you when he started the company, what the

software does, but I never asked him about the name of the company."

"Google, woman. Find out where he works."

I slide into my car, and casually look in the rearview mirror. The creeper appears to me a blonde man, but I'm not sure about the man part. He has a beard, but if he didn't, I'd swear it was a woman.

Weird and did I mention creepy?

I turn out of the lot, telling Bree what I know about Jack's company so that she can search the internet for any hint of where I can find him. "Text me the name when you figure it out."

When the creeper gets in the car and starts following, I get concerned.

"I have some weirdo following me. I'm trying to decide if I should go home or to the police station." I didn't mean to say all that out loud and panic Bree.

"What? Do not hang—"

I realize I cut her off after ending the call, but I need to think right now.

Going straight home just lets the person know where I live, and that's dumb. So I pass my street and turn down the next one without using my blinker, which feels very wrong. Then I wind my way through the neighborhood until I'm sure I'm no longer being followed. Then I go home.

And I call my office, letting them know I won't be in until after lunch.

First, I need to go find Jack.

CHAPTER 18

JACK

I'm pacing in my office. I've gotten zero work done since getting home. Without my phone, I can't log into anything that requires two-factor authentication. I also can't buy anything because my credit card is in my phone case, which is in Sofie's car.

But the part that has me sick is that I can't call Sofie. And I don't know where she lives.

Pete knocks, then pushes open the door. "Hey, Jack."

"Can this wait? I'm not really—"

"Hannah says that it absolutely cannot wait. And that you need to go outside right now." He pulls the phone away from his ear and winces. "Like for real now, she says."

I grab my coat, praying she found out something that will help me find Sofie.

When I get outside, Hannah is in her car, waiting by the double doors. "Get in!"

"Why do you have a beard?" I buckle my seat belt.

She steps on the gas, then stops. "I need to get this thing off. It itches. How do you even survive November?"

"I don't know. Mine doesn't itch. Now can you please tell

me why you ordered me down here and why you have a beard stuck to your face?"

She grabs the edge of the beard, gives a quick tug, and screams. "That was unpleasant."

"Hannah, I've barely slept or eaten in days. My fuse is short and on fire. Please tell me what's going on."

"I'm sorry you've had such a rough few days."

"Don't apologize. Just tell me." I pull in a calming breath, hoping the one thousandth time is a charm. "It's been days, and by now, Sofie either thinks I'm dead or that I ghosted her. Not good. Very bad."

She starts driving.

"Where are we going?"

"First to the coffee shop, but I'll be super quick. I ordered and paid, but I walked out without our cups. But I'll get to why in a minute." She gets on the freeway, and I close my eyes. After I get my car back, I'm never riding with Hannah again. The woman scares me.

"Anytime now is good."

"Okay, so remember when you were telling me about the week and realized you didn't have your phone, so you called it, thinking Sofie would notice it vibrating?" She spends more time looking at me than at the road.

I open my eyes because I don't trust her enough to keep my eyes closed. "Cars! Watch the cars. And yes, I remember. And I remember that I couldn't locate my phone since I turned off location sharing in case my mom tried to track my whereabouts. Yes, Hannah, I remember all that."

"Maybe you shouldn't have coffee."

"Hannah Nichols!"

She laughs. "I'm joking about the coffee. Anyway, I know why she didn't hear it vibrating."

"Do you?"

She bobs her head as she exits the highway. "It's because

she was already out of her car." Without using a blinker, she turns into the coffee place. "Be right back."

I want to scream because Sofie is way more important than coffee.

Ninety-three seconds later, Hannah climbs back into the car and hands me a cup. "It might be a little cold. Sorry."

"Tell me about Sofie. How do you know she was out of her car?"

She passes our complex. "So I saw someone in the coffee shop earlier who looked a lot like Sofie. She was upset about something and was talking on the phone. I didn't want her to know it was me snooping on her because stalking is weird, but luckily, I had that beard and the glue in my purse from that party the other night."

"What part—never mind, I don't want to know. Tell me about Sofie."

Hannah turns into a neighborhood. As she stops along the curb, she points at a house. "She lives right there."

I launch out of the car and run to the door. "Sofie! It's me. Open the door." I knock a few hundred times, but no one answers. And there isn't a car in the driveway either.

At this time of day, she's probably at work. I run back to Hannah's car. "I need to figure out where she works."

"We've had this conversation. And you called how many law offices, asking for her?"

"Seven, but there are way more law offices in Houston than that. Take me back to the office, I'll use your phone and call around some more."

'Wouldn't it just be easier to camp on her porch? I'll bring you food, and you can just wait. Two arrows make for a really hard game of archery. But if you have a non-moving target and one moving arrow, the game is way more fun."

I can see the logic in what she's saying, but waiting feels like torture. "Bring me a cheeseburger and a large Dr Pepper.

And fries. Lots of fries." Striding toward the porch, I say, "And please be careful on the road. I'm terrified you're going to hit something or hurt yourself."

She grins. "You worry too much."

Ten minutes later, Hannah is back, and I'm curious what fast-food worker she talked into making a cheeseburger and fries during breakfast hours. But Hannah could probably talk anyone into anything if she had enough time.

"I have work to do, but I'll come check on you later. Need anything?"

"Sofie."

"Patience. She'll be home eventually."

Any neighbors watching must think I'm nutty, but burglars don't camp out on porches in plain sight. I lean against the front door and stare at the street. How long will I have to wait for her to get home?

* * *

THE LITTLE SLEEP I've had since getting back has been full of strange and chaotic dreams. But this one is a doozy. Bree is shouting, "Please don't be dead" which makes no sense at all.

But the best way to handle crazy dreams and wake up without forgetting them is to act like it's real. So I ask, "Who's dead?"

I'm trying to open my eyes, but my eyelids feel glued shut.

Rubbing my face helps me shake the dream, and when I open my eyes, Bree is grinning at me. "You're alive."

I look from Bree to Zeke, who is standing next to her. "What are y'all doing here?"

"Don't panic, okay?" Bree holds up her hand. "Some creep was following Sofie, and she wasn't sure if she should drive home. She hung up in the middle of our call just like she did when she thought she'd hit you. One day, I'm going to hang up on her, and she's not going to like it."

I hate that Hannah scared Sofie. "It wasn't a creep. Just my friend. And I know she didn't mean to scare Sofie. Hannah just wanted me to be able to find her."

Zeke narrows his eyes. "So she's not in danger?"

"Not that I know of. Her car isn't here, so she's either gone or parked in the garage and ignoring me."

"Bree, call your sister." Zeke steps closer. "Why didn't you call her?"

"My phone is in her car." I've spent so much time worrying about Sofie that I haven't even thought about my car. "Did Chewy call me? He probably thinks I'm ignoring him."

"He'll get over it." Zeke sits beside me on the front step, tension leaving his muscles. "I've never been so worried."

"You finally answered your phone." Bree puts a finger to her lips, then puts the call on speaker.

Sofie's voice comes through the line. "Sorry. I dropped it a while ago when I was driving, and I didn't hear it vibrating. What's up?"

"Where are you?" Bree bounces on the balls of her feet. She's either excited or cold. Or both.

Sofie yawns. "Excuse me. Sorry. I'm camped out in the parking lot next door to Jack's office. From my parking space, I can see the doors. When I went up there earlier, they said he was out. So when he gets back, I'll see him. And tackle him. Then kiss him. Or maybe I'll kiss him first."

"Why don't you leave your number with the front desk and just come back to the house?" Bree pinches her lips, trying not to laugh.

"Wait. What? You said *come* to the house. Where are you?"

"Outside your house. You tell me someone is following you, then hang up on me. When I told dad, we made a quick trip over. But trying to get the trip into the record books might mean trouble for Dad, so we'll have to keep quiet about the record-breaking speed."

"I'm so sorry. I think it was just a homeless person or something. Except they had a car. I don't know, but I haven't seen them since. And I guess I'll come home. Dad has a key. Just go inside. I'll be there in about ten minutes."

Right now, that feels like an eternity.

CHAPTER 19

SOFIE

I set my phone on the center console, then head home. Calling out of work today wasn't what I planned, but now I'm glad I did. But I feel horrible for scaring Dad and Bree.

Traffic stops ahead of me, and I slam on the brakes. My phone goes skittering off somewhere into the back seat just like it did earlier, but I'll grab it when I get home.

As I drive, I'm trying to hear the tiny voice in my head, the one saying Jack didn't ghost me. I'm also hoping that voice has a good explanation for why Jack has been going to and from work but hasn't called me.

When I finally see him, he can explain himself after I kiss him. Because that's what I want to do first.

Once I get home, I reach into the back to get my phone, but I can't find it. So I get out and open the back door. There are two phones on the floorboard. Mine and Jack's.

I slide in behind the wheel and call Bree.

"Hey. What's up?"

"Make yourselves at home. I'm going back to Jack's office.

His phone has been in my car this whole time. So I'm just going to wait for him."

"Sofia Clara De Los Santos, do not hang up the phone. Come inside right now." Bree can be a bit of a dictator sometimes. But delaying my trip back to Jack's office by a few minutes probably won't make that big a difference.

"Okay, but just for a few minutes." I grab my purse and walk to the door.

It swings open before I grab the handle.

Jack, who looks like he's pulled an all-nighter, is standing in the doorway. "Sorry I didn't call you, but my phone fell out in your car, and I didn't know where you lived. Or the name of the law firm where you worked. I called around and even left a message at one place, but I guess there's more than one Sofie De Los Santos that's an attorney here in town." He steps closer. "I hope you didn't think that I was avoiding you. I wasn't. The last two days have been—"

I interrupt him with a kiss. The days have been torture. I can't believe I thought he ghosted me.

When we break out kiss, Bree clears her throat. "I have some questions and something that needs to be said."

I glance behind me as a car pulls up to the curb. "That's the creeper's car. Quick. Close the door." I run behind Jack.

But he doesn't slam that door. He opens it further as a tall willowy blonde makes her way up the walk.

She waves when she gets to the door. "Hi."

Jack moves me in front of him but keeps his arms around me. "Sofie, this is Hannah. Hannah, this is my girlfriend, Sofie."

"It's so nice to meet you, and I am so sorry about earlier. I never meant to scare you." She waves again, but this time it's directed at Dad and Bree. "Hello, Hallmark family."

Bree laughs. "Okay, Hannah, you're awesome. Jack, I want

to know why you didn't you just message me or Sofie on social media."

He scratches his head. "I keep my personal stull off my work laptop, and the charger to my personal laptop must've fallen out in my car because I don't have it, so I couldn't get into that stuff on my laptop, and I didn't have my phone. That's why. Plus, I didn't think of that until you said it."

She rolls her eyes. "And Sofie, you need some local friends who will talk you off the ledge. Seriously."

Hannah raises her hand. "I volunteer!"

I nod. "You are right. And, Hannah, I'd like that. I've heard nothing but good things about you."

Jack whispers loudly, "Because I haven't told you about her driving."

Dad checks the time. "I need to get back." He pulls me into a hug. "Don't hang up on your sister anymore please."

"I'm really sorry about that."

He looks at Jack and motions outside. The two of them stop halfway down the walk to have their little chat. Just far enough away that I can't hear what they're saying. Well, what Dad's saying. Jack is doing a lot of nodding.

Bree gives me a hug. "Looks like I was right."

I'm not giving her the satisfaction of agreeing. "You thought he was dead."

"You might need to explain that to Jack. When I saw him slumped on your porch, I ran up and shouted, 'Please don't be dead!' which, you know, might have weirded him out." She shifts beside me so that we're both watching the conversation out front. "But I was almost right about him. His phone was dead. Slight difference."

I give her a side hug. "I'm sorry for hanging up and not listening to your wisdom."

"I forgive you." She lifts her eyebrows as Jack walks back

toward us. "I'll call you later for a full update." Then she follows Dad to the truck and climbs in.

Jack steps behind me, and I lean against him, watching as Dad and Bree pull away. "I wish they could've stayed longer."

"We can invite them back for a visit. They can pack a bag, bring a toothbrush. You know, all that good stuff."

"I'm sorry I thought you ghosted me." I'm hoping it won't hurt his feelings to hear me say it out loud.

"You can herd cattle, make tamales, and write legal briefs. Only a complete fool would ghost you, Sofie. Seriously." He drops a kiss on my neck. "Have dinner with me."

"I'm going to go, um, do anything else I can think of. This is awkward. Bye!" Hannah rushes down the walkway.

I feel guilty that I forgot she was there. "I like Hannah."

"I'm glad. Now what about dinner?"

I turn so that I'm facing him. "I need to go back to my office. I have several things that need to get done because I've been running around trying to find you. It might be late by the time my stuff is finished."

"I am going to charge my phone, and when your work is complete, call me. I will meet you here with dinner."

"Deal."

He kicks the front door closed. "But before you go…"

In one swift motion he scoops me up and carries me to the couch. "Two weeks ago, I didn't know you. And I had just a regular mostly happy life. Then I met you and my definition of happy completely changed. But these last few days, being apart from you made me feel like I was being deprived of air."

I tug him closer. "A little mouth to mouth will help with that."

* * *

Now that I want to gush about Jack, I'm avoiding my coworkers for an entirely different reason. The sooner I finish my tasks, the sooner I'll see Jack again. I march past the receptionist's desk, looking at my phone so that he won't strike up a conversation.

"Sofie, I have a message for you that came in this morning." Luke quirks an eyebrow. "It was a strange one. I'm thinking not business related."

I hold out my hand. "Now you have me curious."

He hands over a slip of paper, then says the message out loud. "Some guy named Jack said there is no bright side to not seeing you. Sounds like you broke his heart. Should I ignore future calls?"

"No. If he calls again, put him straight through." Once I get to my desk, I tap out a text to Jack.

Me: I got your message. I'll work hard and fast so we can have dinner before midnight.

Jack: It doesn't matter what time. Call me when you're leaving.

I send a heart in reply. It is way too soon to use a specific L-word, so a heart will have to do.

With my office door closed, I get to work, channeling my giddiness into productivity.

Hours later, I tuck three files in my drawer and set one in the middle of my desk to discuss with one of the partners tomorrow. It felt good to be able to focus on work, not as an escape from thinking about Jack, but the way I used to.

As I walk out to my car, I call him.

He answers on the first ring. "Hello, Miss De Los Santos."

"I'm leaving my office now. But since I have a car and you don't, why don't I go to your apartment?"

"Are you still wearing that bright blue suit and those spiky gold heels?"

"Yes, and they're slingbacks, not spiky." I slide in behind the wheel.

He laughs. "They're hot is what they are. I'm in apartment two ten. Just up the stairs from where you dropped me off earlier today."

"I'm on my way. Mind if we talk while I drive?"

"I'd be disappointed if we didn't. How does Thai food sound?"

"Great." I flip on my blinker before blending into traffic. "Order me whatever. Just not too spicy."

"Surprises. Fun. I'm ordering a bunch because I haven't been eating much these last few days, and now that I found you, I'm starved. I'd say I could eat a horse, but then I picture NayNay and feel guilty just thinking the words." He sighs. "I missed my phone almost as much as I missed you. I just ordered on my app, and it was so easy."

We continue to chat as I'm walking to his apartment. When I knock, he says, "Oh, food's here. How far away are you?"

"Not far." I smile as he opens the door. "Not far at all."

CHAPTER 20

JACK

Bandit has spent the last half hour staring at Sofie. I got him after my last breakup, so he's had limited contact with people. His world is mostly Hannah and I. Sofie is new and different.

And my cat is as fascinated with her as I am.

After we finish eating, she drapes her legs over my lap. "This is what I was picturing things would be like when we got back to Houston."

"We're definitely on the same page there. I just wasn't expecting those heels. Wow." I am harping on her shoes a bit, but after spending a week with the Christmasy cowgirl version of Sofie, this put-together lawyer side is a bit of a shock. In a good way. She's both adorable and stunning. It's like finding an extra prize at the bottom of the cereal box or an extra toy in a Happy Meal.

Her musical laugh rings out. "Why do you keep talking about my heels?"

"When I met you, you were in flats. Casual. The next morning you walked into the kitchen in your pajamas with your boots on, and my heart skittered a bit. And now this. You're like a runway model."

She shakes her head. "I am way too short to be a model. But I'm glad you like my array of footwear."

Bandit jumps up and snuggles on her lap.

"He likes you. But he'd be stupid not to." While she gives Bandit the attention he demands, I dance kisses on her jawline. "I saw how hard it was for you to say goodbye to your dad and Bree both times, so I'm curious why you live so far away."

Still petting the cat, she rests her head on my shoulder. "I absolutely love my family. One hundred percent. No questions. But that life—herding cows, feeding chickens—is not what I want. I enjoy it when I'm there. Then I come home, wear fancy shoes, and eat foods from all over the world. The life I want involves pastures and boots only in small doses. Does that make sense?"

"It does." I shift her legs out of my lap. "It's late, and you have to work tomorrow, so I'm sending you home."

"*Sending* me?"

"Don't make me beg." I clasp her hand and lead her toward the door. "I promised your father that I would watch out for you. And that I would memorize your number." I rattle it off so that she can see I took his advice seriously. "Tomorrow, if you aren't otherwise engaged, I'd love to have dinner with you again."

"Yes, then on Saturday, I'm driving you to get your car." She slides into her heels, which makes the height gap slightly less. She stretches up on her tiptoes and gives me a peck. "I'm sorry your family treated you the way they did, but I'm happy I almost hit you."

"You and me both. Now go home." I wink. "Please."

After one more kiss, we walk to her car.

"If you want to invite Hannah to dinner, I'm okay with that."

I'm not sure I'm ready to share Sofie's attention with anyone other than Bandit after being deprived of it for days. "Maybe. We'll see. I was thinking I'd heat up those tamales you sent home with me."

"Perfect. I'll make rice."

"Just let me know what groceries I need to have on hand. And please text or call when you make it home. Because if you don't, I'll be forced to walk over there. And it's late and cold."

"Look at you being all protective."

I puff up my chest. "Yes, ma'am." I add extra drawl, doing my best to sound like Colt.

Sofie laughs as she gets in the car. "Give me five minutes." After blowing me a kiss, she pulls out of the lot.

I'm nuts if I think I need this routine to go on for days or weeks to solidify my feelings.

Crazy as it sounds, I love Sofie. I've learned so much in the short time we've known each other. Like why all those sweet romantic movies are set in small towns. The possibility of not finding someone doesn't exist.

And if it weren't for family and meddling friends, I'm not sure how long it would've taken me to find Sofie.

* * *

INSTEAD OF DRIVING to the ranch, I booked us two tickets, and we flew to San Antonio. Bree picked us up from the airport, enormously proud of herself for convincing her dad to let her do it on her own.

I don't envy that man.

Sofie is headstrong and independent. But Bree is double that.

I picked up my car, and we spent two amazing days at the ranch.

And on Sunday, we waited until the last minute to leave. Now, we're an hour from home. Sofie is sound asleep, but her fingers are laced with mine.

She mumbles something.

"What's that, sweetie?" I'm using pet names. I don't think I've ever called a woman something other than their name or a variation thereof.

She squeezes my hand and shifts in her seat, her eyes still closed. "Love you, Jack."

"I love you too, Sofie." After hearing those words from her lips, I feel a bit like I'm dreaming too.

* * *

TWO MONTHS LATER, my dad is standing outside my apartment when I get home. To say I'm surprised is an understatement because I haven't heard from anyone in my family since Mom's threatening text. "Hi, Dad. What's up?"

"I owe you an apology."

Shocked, I drop my keys. "Oh?"

"I shouldn't have kept quiet while your mother tried to convince you that your brother's cheating and stealing wasn't a big deal. Just a mistake, as she calls it." He crosses his arms, bothered by something. "It was the worst kind of betrayal. I was disappointed but kept quiet because of your mother. I'm not sure why she can't see what he's become."

"Did something happen?"

"Will and Lynette stole a couple of the family heirlooms I had on display in my office, the pocket watch and the antique spyglass. They needed money to fund some trip they were planning."

"Dad, I'm sorry. I know those meant a lot to you."

He nods. "Thankfully, I tracked them to a pawn shop and bought them back. But that's not really why I'm here. I came to apologize and see if I could take you to dinner."

"Sure. But I need to call my girlfriend because we had plans."

"Bring her along. I'd love to meet her." He shifts his stance and shoves his hands in his pockets. "Your mother and I are getting divorced, Jack. When I pressed charges on Will and Lynette, your mother left me. And I don't want to have burned every bridge in my life. Some I didn't set fire to. I just watched as others did, but the end result is the same. It's up to me to rebuild bridges where I can."

"Dad, I—"

"Please tell me I'm not too late."

"You aren't. Dinner is a good start. And I think you'll love Sofie. I do."

He smiles at me like he's proud of me, something I've wished for a long time.

Before I can even send off a text, Sofie walks up and extends her hand. "Hi, I'm Sofie." She's in one of her fitted suits, and today she's in red heels, hands down my favorite pair.

"Harold Hastings. A pleasure to meet you." He nods in my direction. "I'm Jack's dad."

A caution light flashes behind her eyes, but her smile doesn't falter. "What a nice surprise."

I put an arm around her. "Dad would like to take us to dinner. Is that okay with you?"

In a split second of eye contact, she accesses the situation. "Yes. Absolutely. That's very kind of you, Mr. Hastings."

I'm happy that Dad came around, but it might be best if Sofie never meets my mother.

* * *

It's a hot day in July when I sneak away from Houston to meet Zeke for a late breakfast. Neither of us have discussed why I want to talk to him in person, but we both know. He has to know.

I slide into the wooden booth in the small-town diner. "Is this place new?"

"Yep. Just opened a month ago. And it's ten minutes from the house. Food is good."

"Awesome. Thanks for meeting me. I came because..." I inhale, trying to remember my rehearsed request. "During the drive over, I planned out what I was going to say, but I can't remember any of it. So, um." I drag my palms on my pant legs, nervous. "Okay, here goes. I love Sofie. A lot. She's kind and smart. Beautiful and talented. And I want to spend the rest of my life with her. It would mean the world to me—and also to Sofie once she finds out—if you gave us your blessing."

"You have it, Jack. I have no doubt that my daughter loves you, and it's obvious that you love her just as much. Have you bought a ring?"

"I have. But..." I thread my fingers through my hair, embarrassed that I have to admit my predicament. "I had it out one night because when she's not there, I just stare at it, trying to decide what to say when I ask. But anyway, one night, I turned around for a second, and my cat stole it. I've been searching my apartment high and low, and I can't find it. But if I don't find it by Friday when we're headed to the ranch for the Fourth, I'll just go buy a new one."

"Your cat, huh?"

"His name is Bandit."

Zeke laughs and picks up his menu. "Where do you plan to propose?"

"In the barn. I was going to go help her feed the horses and then drop to one knee." I stare at the words on the menu, too exhilarated to process the meaning. "Too silly?"

"She'll love it."

"I hope so." I just need to find that blasted ring.

CHAPTER 21

SOFIE

Hannah tosses my bag in the back seat of her car. "Jack was busy, so I volunteered to come get you."

"Busy with what?" I buckle my seat belt. This is my first time riding with Hannah, and Jack has warned me about her driving. But it's a short drive.

"He's tearing apart his apartment, looking for something. His cat is a thief." She flicks the blinker, then turns out of the neighborhood.

"So I've heard." I suppose I'll be helping Jack search when I get there. Because the sooner he finds whatever he's hunting for, the quicker we can get on the road. I'm excited about going to the ranch. It's been months since my last visit, and I'm ready for some of that fresh air.

Hannah pulls into her reserved spot. "I hope y'all have a fabulous time at the ranch. It sounds like an awesome place."

A lightbulb goes off in my head. "You should come with us."

"Me?" She points at herself. "On a ranch?"

"Sure! You'd have fun. Please come with us." I get out of the car and grab my bag. "You won't regret it."

"But I'll be a third wheel. Jack wants to spend time with you."

"You aren't a third wheel. Jack and I see each other every single day. But if it makes you feel better, I'll ask his opinion."

She nods. "If he says it's okay, then I'll go."

I rush up the stairs and let myself into the apartment. "I'm here."

Jack is stretched out on his side, shining a flashlight under the TV cabinet. "Hi, sweetie. I'm packed, but give me a few minutes because I'm trying to find something that Bandit stole."

"I'll help you look." I kick off my shoes. "What do you think about Hannah coming with us to the ranch?"

"I think it would be a blast, but I'm not sure the rural parts of Texas are ready for Hannah."

"Hey! I heard that." Hannah crosses her arms.

Jack laughs. "You should come along."

"I can't believe I'm doing this. I'll go pack. Don't leave without me." She hurries out the door.

I stretch out on the floor beside Jack. "I have another idea. But it requires an AirTag and a shoelace."

He rolls to his side, facing me. "I'm listening."

"We put an AirTag on a shoelace and leave it on the table. Then we go in the kitchen and ignore it for a few minutes. Maybe Bandit will take the bait, and it will lead us to his stash."

"You are so smart, and I'm massively attracted to you right now." He pushes off the floor. "And luckily, I have an AirTag."

He sets the trap, and then we sneak off to the kitchen and take turns peeking into the living room. We trade stories about how our days went, and when we notice that the shoelace is no longer on the table, we begin the hunt.

The AirTag chirps, and I follow the sound. "It sounds like it's coming from the couch."

"I've looked under it a hundred times." Jack sighs. "Bandit, what have you done with my stuff, dude?"

Bandit pokes his head out of a hole in the seam of the couch.

"Jack, have you looked *in* the couch? Because that's where Bandit is currently."

"He tore the couch? You little destructive beast." Then my normally calm and logical boyfriend tears the seam even more.

Laces, earbuds, and other trinkets tumble out of the sofa, but I'm focused on the silver chain with the heart-shaped locket at the end. "My locket. I've been looking for it. I couldn't remember where's I'd taken it off, and it broke my heart to think I'd lost it."

"I didn't know he'd stolen that."

I open it so that Jack can see his picture on one side and the group selfie we took after making cookies on the other. "I love this locket."

"I thought you were looking at the other shiny thing that fell out of the sofa." Jack drops to one knee. "Sofia Clara De Los Santos, I had a grand plan to sneak out to the horse barn with you for a few stolen kisses like when we first met and then I'd get down on one knee like this and tell you that meeting you is the most amazing thing that's happened to me, and that being around you is to my heart what air is to my lungs. But Bandit sort of messed that all up." He holds out a ring that has an oval diamond nestled between two clusters of tiny diamonds. "I love you with every atom of my being. And more than anything else in the world, I want to spend every single day of my life with you. Will you marry me, Sof?"

"Yes, Jack. Nothing would make me happier." I hold out my shaking hand for him to slide the ring onto my finger.

Then he scoops me into his arms. "I'm sorry it's not what I planned."

"I love that it's just us."

He sits down on the couch, still holding me. "I love that I'm in your locket. You and me, we were meant to be."

"I agree."

We kiss until Hannah returns.

Jack winks and whispers, "Let's see how long it takes her to notice."

He loads our bags, and we make the drive to the ranch. And Hannah never mentions the ring.

But when we arrive at the Rocking Double Heart Ranch, as soon as I step out of the car, Bree screams, "A ring!"

Dad smiles his approval.

Then Bree, Dad, Hannah, Jack, and I share a group hug.

This is going to be an amazing visit.

EPILOGUE

BREE

I slam on my brakes. Megan Hope, star of five romcoms and one of my favorite actresses is walking down the side of the road in a wedding dress.

She hurries her pace, which hurts my feelings a little. But then I realize she doesn't know it's a sixteen-year-old girl driving this big old truck. So I roll down the window. "Hello!"

Megan stops and flashes a nervous smile. "Hi. I seem to have gotten myself a little lost."

Her face is red like she's been crying, and if Sofie were here, she'd drag Megan back to the house and feed her. So that's what I'll do.

"I can give you a ride."

She makes her way to the truck and climbs in. "Thank you so much. I'm Me—"

"Oh, I know who you are, but don't worry. I won't go all fan girl on you. But I am a fan. A huge one!" I stick out my hand. "I'm Bree."

"So very nice to meet you, Bree."

"Is there somewhere you need to be? Or I can take you

back to my house if you want to hide for a bit. You seem a bit upset."

Megan wipes her eyes. "Honestly, disappearing sounds like a wonderful idea."

I drive her back to the ranch, and sigh when I see that Dad's truck isn't here. He'll just worry. And he shouldn't. When Sofie picked up someone off the side of the road, it worked out really well, so I don't see why he'd complain about this.

"This is where I live. The Rocking Double Heart Ranch. How long have you been walking?"

"Hours. We were filming, and—never mind. It's not important. But it's nice to not be looking over my shoulder."

"Make yourself at home." I walk her into Dad's room because Sofie has all her wedding stuff in her room. "My dad won't be home for a while, but you can shower in here. And feel free to grab one of his shirts or whatever. I'm not sure you'd fit in my shirts because..." I glance down at my chest and hope she understands.

A quizzical expression has her brow knitted.

So I explain further. "Your girls are bigger than my girls. But I have some leggings you could borrow. I'll put them on the bed."

"Awesome. Thank you."

"While you shower, I'll make us something to eat. Take your time." I walk into the kitchen and turn up the stereo as I pull ingredients out of the fridge and start cooking.

Dad cooks more than I do, but I'm not a horrible cook. And everyone eats spaghetti, right? I grab the huge bowl of tomatoes Dad harvested from his garden this morning and slide them into the oven to roast.

I'm making dinner for Megan Hope. Pinch me now.

Listening to music, I lose track of time.

"Bree!" Dad does not sound happy.

I open my arms to hug him when he walks into the kitchen, but he waves me off.

"Why is there a woman in my bedroom?" His tone indicates that maybe something happened.

"That's Megan. I told her she could shower in your room."

He lowers his voice as footsteps sound in the hall. "That would've been good to know before I barged in there. You have to tell me these things, Bree."

Megan walks into the kitchen wearing my leggings and one of Dad's shirts. "I'm so sorry I startled you."

"It's fine." Dad is doing his darnedest not to look at Megan, which makes no sense because she looks super cute in his shirt.

Or maybe he noticed how cute she is, and that's why he's not looking at her.

This is so exciting. Later I'm going to call Sofie, tell her that Dad met someone and then just hang up. My sister totally deserves that.

"I made spaghetti. The sauce is made from Dad's tomatoes and the basil he grows. It smells amazing. It'll be ready in just a few minutes. Like ten. Y'all can just talk while I cook."

Dad shoots me a look, but I just smile.

"Offer her a drink, Dad. Be polite."

He gives a grunt, and I'm quite sure he and I will have a chat later. And I'll ask him what he thinks of Megan. Even though it's kind of obvious.

He pours her a glass of wine, and they go sit in the living room.

Sofie is never going to believe this.

* * *

Keep Reading for a BONUS Epilogue!

BONUS EPILOGUE

JACK

I open one eye as Gracelyn climbs over me to snuggle between Sofie and me. Clarabelle is stretched out above our heads, kicking me anytime she rolls over. Bandit is curled up on my feet, so I dare not move them or risk getting a toe gnawed on.

Sofie rolls to her side and rubs Gracelyn's back, buying us a little more time before it's time to open presents.

My beautiful wife blows me a kiss, and even though I'm sleep-deprived, all is right with the world.

Sofie finds my hand in the covers, and fingers linked, we both drift back to sleep.

An hour later, my eyelids are being lifted. "Daddy, Santa came. We need to wake up." Gracelyn smiles. "Clarabelle is waking Mommy."

At least I'm not the only one getting my eyes peeled open.

I yawn and roll out of bed. "Y'all stay here. I'll see if he's come already."

The girls bounce on the bed. "Hurry, Daddy."

Having little humans call me Daddy gives me the same

feeling, or a similar feeling, to when Sofie whispers "I love you."

I quickly get the coffee brewing, then rush back to the bedroom. "There are so many presents!"

Clarabelle launches herself at me, not doubting that I'll catch her. "Let's go see!"

Gracelyn runs out of the room. "I'm going to wake up Grandpa."

Halfway down the hall, she starts squealing.

Sofie laughs. "At least he'll hear her coming."

So much has changed in the seven years since Sofie skidded into my life. But some things haven't changed, like how much I love spending Christmas with her family. Although, her family is bigger now than it used to be.

I give Sofie a good-morning kiss. "I started the coffee. But we need to get some before Bree downs an entire pot. Your sister guzzles coffee like a mad woman."

When we get to the living room, the girls are patiently jumping up and down beside the tree. It's the same tree Bree set up the first Christmas I was here, and those lights are still working.

I sit on the couch, distracting the girls until Zeke, Megan, and Bree make it to the living room.

Then Sofie hands me coffee before easing down beside me. "After this, I think we should go out and feed the horses."

"Yes, please." There have been a whole lot of horses added to the ranch. It doesn't take long to feed them, but I'm sure it'll take us at least an hour. Maybe longer if I can find us somewhere cozy to cuddle up.

"My uncles are all coming for lunch, so it'll get chaotic after that."

"Think we'll survive?" I wink.

"Only if we stick together." She kisses my cheek as the others join us.

Bree plops down beside her nieces. "Merry Christmas! It's time to open gifts."

Gracelyn wags her head back and forth. "Not without Grandpa."

Zeke walks in, wearing a Santa hat. "Did someone call me?"

Clarabelle claps. "He's here. Now we can open gifts." She runs to Megan and drags her to the tree. "Grammy, you sit by me."

We're all in flannel pajamas, but they're all different, which is exactly how I like it.

A NOTE TO READERS

Thank you for reading!

I hope you loved this little holiday treat. The idea for Rocking Double Heart Ranch has been nodding around in my head, and this seemed like a fun way to introduce readers to the ranch. And Zeke. He'll lead off the series.

Be sure to check out my website for updates about new series and for information about my other books. You can also subscribe and get exclusive epilogues and stories.

www.PhreyPress.com

ALSO BY REMI CARRINGTON

Cowboys of Stargazer Springs

The ranch hands on Stargazer Springs Ranch find love. Sometimes in unexpected ways.

Stargazer Spring Ranch

Love after forty still happens on and around Stargazer Springs Ranch.

Never Say Never series

Several first responders and a swoon-worthy cowboy each finds love in this rom com series.

Bluebonnets & Billionaires series

Swoon-worthy heroes with lots of money (& even more heart) will have you sighing, laughing, and falling in love.

* * *

Pamela Humphrey, who writes as Remi Carrington, also releases books under her own name. Visit PhreyPress.com for more information about her books.

ABOUT THE AUTHOR

Remi Carrington is a figment of Pamela Humphrey's imagination. She loves romance & chocolate, enjoys disappearing into a delicious book, and considers people-watching a sport. She was born in the pages of the novel *Just You* and then grew into an alter ego.

She writes sweet romance and romantic comedies set in Texas. Her books are part of the Phrey Press imprint.

facebook.com/remiromance
instagram.com/phreypress

Made in the USA
Coppell, TX
05 November 2024

39669575R00090